Octopus
Encounter

OTHER BOOKS BY SALLY STREIB

The Heart Mender
Summer of the Sharks
Treasures by the Sea

Octopus Encounter

SALLY STREIB

Pacific Press® Publishing Association
Nampa, Idaho
Oshawa, Ontario, Canada
www.pacificpress.com

Cover design by Gerald Lee Monks
Cover illustration by Marcus Mashburn

Copyright 2007 by
Pacific Press® Publishing Association
Printed in the United States of America

ISBN 13: 978-0-8163-2210-7
ISBN 10: 0-8163-2210-4

You can obtain additional copies of this book by calling toll-free
1-800-765-6955 or by visiting http://www.adventistbookcenter.com.

07 08 09 10 11 • 5 4 3 2 1

DEDICATION

To my brothers Bob and Glenn Wilcox,
who played the role of father to me as a child
and who have listened to and laughed at my wild tales.
They helped me go down into the sea,
where I experienced the adventures in this book.

The events in this book are true adventures
the author had as she dived into and explored
the sea around Grand Cayman Island in 2004 and 2006.
Susan and Eric represent the many kids
who have joined her on these adventures.

CONTENTS

CHAPTER 1

A NEW ADVENTURE

Susan awoke with a start. For a moment, she wondered where she was. Then she heard the pounding of waves against the foot of the cliff just below the house. She sat up, pulled her long brown hair back with her hands, and tied it with a ribbon that she grabbed from her nightstand.

She ran to the window and gazed out at the water. A big wave surged forward and smashed against the rocks, tumbling over them and flying up as foam. Then it gathered itself together and withdrew into the great ocean beyond.

Susan looked down the face of the cliff. Palm trees marched along the beach, their fronds swaying in the breeze. Diamonds of light danced in the pools of water caught among the rocks and the white sands of Laguna Beach, California. "I'm home!" she called out. But even as she realized how glad she was to stand by her own bedroom window, she felt a pang of sorrow. She had just spent a whole month with Aunt Sally; Uncle Merle; her twin brother, Eric; and Kevin, Eric's friend, on Eleuthera, the island of freedom in the Bahamas. She already missed the silky, azure water, the reefs full of rainbow-colored fish, and, most of all, SNUBA diving.

Susan heard the front door fly open, so she ran to a window that overlooked the front of the house. Eric was standing on the front steps, a duffle bag at his feet. He pushed a shock of blond hair off his freckled forehead and watched as a blue Jeep headed up the driveway and stopped. A man wearing khaki shorts and a T-shirt with a dive logo on the front stepped out. His skin looked as brown as leather, and his face crinkled when he smiled, like a pool of water stirred by a breeze. *It's Mr. Wood, the retired marine biologist who was on Eleuthera Island,* Susan thought.

Then a tall, red-haired boy unfolded himself and stood beside the Jeep. "You must be Eric," he said. "I'm Josh, Mr. Wood's lab assistant. He says you'll be working with him from now on. I'm leaving for college next month."

"Hi," Eric said, jamming his hands into his jean pockets.

"You must be a real water creature," Josh continued. "Mr. Wood never hires anyone who doesn't just love to be wet and have a camera in one hand."

"I guess I kind of stumbled into the whole thing," Eric admitted. "I have to blame Mr. Wood and two spotted eagle rays. Mr. Wood came over to borrow some O-rings for his SCUBA tank, and I ended up showing him how to use SNUBA gear."

"I understand SNUBA is a lot like diving," Josh said.

"Yes, except you float your air tank on a small raft instead of carrying it on your back," Eric said. "Showing him how it all works got me into the water. I saw those giant rays just below me. Two of them flew past me like eagles on the wing. They really got my attention."

"So by the time you remembered to be afraid, you'd

already gone down to get a closer look," Josh said, laughing.

"Something like that," Eric replied.

Just then, Aunt Sally appeared at the front door. "Mr. Wood, how are you?" she inquired.

"I'm fine," he said. "It's good to see you again, Sally. How are Merle and Susan?"

"They're just great," Aunt Sally said. "They're both upstairs. Unpacking is our job for today." Then Aunt Sally handed Eric a paper bag and said, "Here, take this lunch with you. I'll pick you up at five o'clock."

"We'll see you then," Mr. Wood said.

Susan watched Eric, Josh, and Mr. Wood climb into the Jeep and drive away. Eric stuck a hand out the side window and waved. *He sure looks happy,* Susan thought— and suddenly she wished she had something that could make her feel as excited as Eric seemed to be. He had learned to talk about his adventures with pictures. He spent a lot of time working to perfect each one. It had become hard to pry him away from the computer unless someone mentioned going out into the water again. Susan felt glad that her twin brother, usually fearful and moody, was changing. But she also felt kind of sad. Eric knew what he wanted to do; he had even given up his place on the baseball team to take a part-time job with Mr. Wood. She remembered him saying, "I'm going to use every spare minute to study the sea."

At the thought, Susan blurted out the words, "What about me?"

"What do you mean, 'what about me?' " Aunt Sally said, coming into Susan's room with an armful of clean clothes.

"I want to feel excited about something, like Eric does," Susan said. "He's changed."

Aunt Sally placed the clothes on Susan's bed. She sat down and pulled Susan onto the bed beside her. "You're right, Susan. That's exactly what your uncle Merle and I hoped would happen to Eric when we invited him to come to the island and help us with the reef replenishment project. It seems that he has not only moved beyond his fears, he's discovering his spiritual gifts."

"What do you mean?" Susan asked.

"Spiritual gifts are abilities that God gives to people who choose to love and serve Him. Discovering their spiritual gifts gives them a sense of purpose and a passion for living."

"You mean that Eric is learning to use his love for the sea and for taking pictures to help people see how good God is? Is that why he's so excited?"

"Exactly," Aunt Sally said, giving Susan a hug.

Susan thought a minute. *Eric does love to sit in front of the computer for hours, poring over one picture. He keeps working until he gets the picture perfect. Then he likes to show others the pictures to help them think about God, their Creator.*

"Eric will learn more and more about using his unique abilities," Aunt Sally continued. "He will discover his mission in life and become more and more focused on it. And in due time, you'll learn about yours too."

"But I don't have any gifts," Susan said, a tear running down her face.

Aunt Sally's cell phone rang, interrupting them. "Yes, Susan is here," she said, handing the phone to Susan.

"Hi!" Susan said. "How's it going? Yes, we had a great time on the island. I almost got eaten by a shark and—

"I can't go today. I have to unpack. I promise I'll go next Sunday. See you at school tomorrow."

Susan closed the phone and handed it to Aunt Sally. "It was Margo, Kevin's sister," Susan explained. "She wanted me to go shopping with her. I don't feel like shopping. I guess I wanted to talk about my adventures."

"I see," Aunt Sally said. They sat in silence for a few moments. "I guess you miss Eleuthera already," Aunt Sally said. "I always feel blue when I have to leave the island. It's hard to get back into the swing of daily events here at home." She stood up and started toward the stairway.

Aunt Sally's right, Susan admitted to herself. She had daydreamed about ways to get back onto an island, any island. She did miss the water. But she wanted to tell Aunt Sally that she felt something else besides just missing the island. She didn't know how to explain it, but she felt restless. *If I could only understand why*, she thought.

Just then the phone rang again. "I'll tell her," Aunt Sally said, hanging up. "Susan, Eric forgot some pictures. He says you'll find them on his computer in a file named RAYS.1. He wants you to copy them onto his flash drive. I'll take the flash drive to him when I go to pick him up. When did you learn how to use a flash drive?" she asked.

"Kevin and Eric taught me when we worked on pictures in Discovery House on Eleuthera. I'll get it ready and bring it down in a few minutes."

"Take your time," Aunt Sally said. "I won't leave until four-thirty."

Susan switched on the computer, located Eric's picture files, and selected RAYS.1.

"Wow!" she said to herself. "These pictures look great." She remembered that Eric had spent hours peering at the computer screen. Then she noticed that Eric had written a short description beneath each picture. She looked at a shot of a ray swimming past Eric. Beneath the photo he had written, "The ray got very close."

"Close!" Susan shouted and then laughed. The ray had touched him! *If I had been there, I'd have stopped breathing*, she thought. She deleted Eric's words and wrote instead, "The ray swooped down and flew past me, its wing brushing my shoulder."

Susan selected another picture. "A ray eating mollusk creatures from some shells," the caption read. *Boring*, Susan thought. Again, she deleted the words, replacing them with "I heard a crack as the ray crushed the milk conch in two and then sucked out the slimy mollusk."

She pulled up the next picture and changed its caption. Then she worked on another, and another, and before she knew it, two hours had passed. Suddenly, she stopped and gasped. *I've changed every caption,* she thought, *and I didn't ask Eric if I could. Maybe he'll be angry*. Then she sighed and said to herself, "Oh, well. It was fun, and the captions sound a lot better." She saved the changes, copied the files, shut down the computer, and ran down the stairs.

Aunt Sally's phone rang again. Susan heard her sigh as she picked it up. *I guess she's having a hard time getting anything done*, she thought.

"It's Eric. He wants to talk with you," Aunt Sally said, handing the phone to Susan.

"Of course I got the files copied correctly," Susan said. She wanted to tease Eric about his boring captions but decided against it.

"Mr. Wood asked me to invite you to help us in the lab next Sunday," Eric said.

"In the lab?" Susan said. She felt a bit of excitement rise within her, but it was mixed with a sense of dread she didn't understand. She handed the phone to Aunt Sally.

"He just wanted to remind me to send the pictures," she said. "I think I'll go with Eric next Sunday if that's OK."

"Go with Eric?" Aunt Sally said, looking at Susan. "I thought you promised to go shopping with Margo."

"I know," Susan mumbled, turning toward the stairs to her room. She paused a minute. "I don't know why," she said, "but I don't feel like doing stuff like that right now."

Susan ran up the stairs and into her room. She opened her bulging suitcase and pulled out rumpled shorts, shirts, and swimsuits, dumping them into a pile on the floor. "I'll never be as good as Eric at editing pictures," she said to herself, "probably because I can't sit still that long. But I can try. It'll be fun," she decided. *Besides, wandering around the mall just doesn't seem exciting. Not when you've spent time hanging out with sharks and eagle rays at the bottom of the sea,* she thought. "Have I changed too?" she wondered out loud.

Susan removed her snorkel gear, placed it in her bathroom sink, and squirted soap into the water. Even though she had cleaned her gear carefully on the island before packing it into her suitcase, she washed each piece again, making sure she removed the remaining salt particles that might cause the rubber to decay. Then she placed them in the tub to dry. She smiled, thinking of the way she had bobbed around in the shallow water the first time she tried to jam her feet into her fins. Then Eric had showed her how to make a loop of each strap, slip her feet in, and pull the straps to tighten them around her ankles. Suddenly, she missed being with Eric. *We always do everything together,* she thought. *But now Eric is going in a new direction. What's my direction?* She sighed.

At 5:30, Eric returned. Susan heard him tumble up the stairs into his room.

"How'd it go?" she said peering through his doorway.

"Fantastic!" Eric said. "Mr. Wood really liked the pictures."

"That's good," Susan said.

"Thanks for sending the files," Eric said, reaching out and yanking Susan's ponytail. "I can't believe you remembered how to copy pictures." He grabbed the suitcase that sat on the floor near the door and dropped it onto his bed. "I guess I ought to get this thing unpacked," he said.

"If you wait any longer to clean that stuff, you'll have an algae garden in your suitcase," Susan said, laughing as she plopped onto Eric's bed. She wanted to ask him how he liked the new captions, but Aunt Sally called them to supper before she got the words out. Eric didn't waste any time getting down stairs and plunking himself onto a chair at the dinner table.

Uncle Merle came into the house, pulling a big suitcase behind him. When he saw the table set up for supper, he dropped the handle and joined Eric and Susan. Aunt Sally brought a tray of tacos to the table.

"Eric, how was your first day with Mr. Wood?" Uncle Merle asked.

"Fantastic!" Eric said, smiling. "Mr. Wood said I'm even more creative than he first thought."

"Fantastic?" Susan blurted. Everyone looked at her. *That's a new one*, she thought. *In the past, Eric would have mumbled an "OK." Now everything's "fantastic!"* She suddenly realized that she felt irritated by Eric's new attitude. Yet she felt glad too.

"Susan's going with me to the institute next week," Eric said, looking at her. "I think she'll like working with the pictures."

Susan squirmed in her chair. Eric liked editing pictures, but she didn't feel sure she would like it.

"Sounds interesting," Uncle Merle said, casting Aunt Sally a glance. Susan saw her eyebrows rise just a little, and she wondered if Aunt Sally was thinking about how hard it was for Susan to sit still for long. But Aunt Sally didn't say anything.

"Mr. Wood said I was a natural photographer, and he really likes my captions," Eric said.

"Your captions? I—" Susan started to say, but just then Uncle Merle stood up and asked, "Are you two sick of island-hopping and snooping around under the sea?"

"Are you kidding?" Eric exclaimed.

"I'm not sick of it," Susan blurted. "I started dreaming of a way to get back to Eleuthera the moment we flew away. Can we go back soon?"

"I'm afraid not—we have other work to do," Uncle Merle said.

Eric and Susan groaned, and twin frowns settled on their faces.

"Tell these knobby-heads the truth," Aunt Sally said, smiling.

Susan stared at Aunt Sally. She remembered again how glad she felt that Aunt Sally and Uncle Merle had invited Eric and her to live with them after their mother had been killed in a terrible accident. She knew that her aunt and uncle loved them. And they both loved the sea. She felt sure there would always be new adventures in her life.

"We can't go back to Eleuthera right now. It's just impossible," Uncle Merle said.

"Merle!" Aunt Sally protested.

"We're not going to Eleuthera, and that's final," Uncle Merle said. "We're going to the Cayman Islands."

"What?" Susan said jumping to her feet. "Did you say we're going to an island?"

"That's right!" Uncle Merle said. "Seven Seas Marine Institute has asked us to spend three weeks on the Cayman Islands during Christmas break. They want us to photograph Babylon Reef and check on how much damage the recent hurricane caused."

"The Cayman Islands!" Susan shrieked, jumping up and dancing around the room. "Another island! More water. More SNUBA diving."

"No more SNUBA diving," Uncle Merle said, trying to look serious.

"But why?" Eric moaned. "I have to get close to take good pictures."

"I'm sorry. No more SNUBA diving."

Susan and Eric shot glances at Aunt Sally, begging her to explain.

"Merle!" Aunt Sally said, her face frowning, but her eyes dancing with some secret joy.

"No more SNUBA diving. You are both ready to SCUBA."

"I'm going to be a real SCUBA diver!" Susan shouted, jumping up again.

"When can we start?" Eric asked, not showing the least sign of fear.

Susan stared at Eric. *He really has changed. He isn't afraid,* she thought. *He wants to dive.*

"I've already made arrangements for you to begin lessons," Aunt Sally said.

"Wow!" Susan gasped. Suddenly, she couldn't eat another bite. There was a lot to do to get ready.

"Sally," Uncle Merle said, "there are some people we need to connect with. Please call Clyde Thomas and his son, Reggie—the guys you dived Grand Cayman with two summers ago. Ask them for some information about good dive sites. And Eric and Susan, you need to let your dad know what new adventure you are up to. We'll need his permission to take you out of the country. While on the island, you can send an e-mail or two."

Eric stared out the window for a long time. Susan thought he might be dreaming of taking his first underwater photo in the Cayman Islands.

"Where is Cayman?" he said, turning to the table again.

"The country of Cayman Islands consists of three small islands located south of Florida and the island of Cuba," Aunt Sally explained. "The three islands are Grand Cayman, Cayman Brac, and Little Cayman. We'll be studying the reefs along the north edge of Grand Cayman, the largest of the three islands."

"This time I'm not breaking a leg or even getting a bruise," Uncle Merle said, laughing.

"You mean you won't miss dragging around that blue cast?" Aunt Sally teased.

"This time I'm going to spend every second in the water," Eric said.

This time, I'm going to keep a detailed notebook so I won't forget anything, Susan thought.

"We have a lot of work to do," Aunt Sally said, standing up and gathering the dirty dishes from the table. "We also have a bunch of equipment to gather."

Here we go again, Susan thought, her restless feelings evaporating. *Here we go!*

CHAPTER 2

DESTINATION: CAYMAN ISLANDS

Susan stared out the window in front of her. A breeze rustled through the palm trees and danced across the green sea. She spotted a pair of binoculars sitting on the window ledge and pushed back an urge to grab them and look into the tide pools that nestled among the rocks clustered at the edge of the sandy beach. Then she sighed. Two hours had passed since Eric and she had arrived at Seven Seas Marine Institute to help Mr. Wood in the lab. She squirmed in her chair.

"Are you working?" Eric asked, glancing over at Susan.

"Of course I am," Susan said, instantly dropping her eyes to the computer screen. "I'm looking at that picture of the nurse shark that Aunt Sally and I almost ran into in the fishermen's cut on Eleuthera Island."

Susan stared at the computer screen and the picture on it of a nurse shark that lay against the rocky wall of the narrow cut. She recognized the shark because of the two barbells that hung down from its upper lip and the two almost same-size dorsal fins on its back.

Eric stretched, walked to Susan's side, and peered over her shoulder. "I don't care what scientists say," he commented. "A shark is a shark. That one looks big enough to do some damage."

"What do the scientists say?" Susan asked.

"They say that the nurse shark is the shark least likely to attack, unless you tease it or grab its fins."

"Good. I don't have to worry about being attacked by one," Susan said.

"Why not?" Eric asked.

"Because I don't plan on ever grabbing the fin of a nurse shark or any other shark," Susan said, looking up at her brother.

Eric laughed. He watched Susan crop away some dark areas that bordered the picture, zoom in to show more detail on the shark's body, and push the save button. "That looks good," he said, returning to his own computer. "Try to go over all thirty shots. Crop off what you see as excess background, and then I'll take a look at them."

Susan nodded agreement and clicked on another picture. A few minutes later, she glanced out the window again. White stucco buildings with red Spanish tile roofs clustered together near the edge of the thirty-foot cliffs. She watched a wave rise up and form a thin, green wall. It trembled a moment and then fell down upon itself, spewing foam into the sky, sweeping up the sandy beach, and tumbling over the rocks that lay at the foot of the cliffs.

Suddenly, Susan spotted a small, black object rolling in a wave. As the water receded, it left the object stranded on the sand. Whatever it was lay still. Susan jumped up and ran to the window. There, she grabbed the binoculars and scanned the beach. Then, putting the binoculars back onto the windowsill and darting for the door, she said, "I've got to take a look at something."

"Come back here," Eric called after her, but Susan kept going. She ran down the hall and out a door that faced the sea. She located a trail and made her way down toward the beach, slipping and sliding in the loose gravel and sand. She could see the black speck below her.

"Maybe it's just an old log," she said to a seagull that swooped past her, squawking. "I have to check it out."

As soon as Susan reached the black object on the beach, she knew it was a baby seal. The little creature didn't move or try to get away. Susan looked toward the window of the lab. Eric stood peering down at her through the binoculars. She jumped up and down, waving her arms. "Come down here, Eric," she cried into the wind. "Hurry up!"

Eric disappeared from the window, and Susan knelt down beside the seal. "Poor little thing," she said.

A few minutes later, Susan heard Eric and Mr. Wood talking as they walked toward her. "I think it's hurt," she shouted to them over the sound of the waves.

When they reached Susan, Mr. Wood bent down and looked at the seal. It had a deep gash on its left side. He reached into his pocket and pulled out a cell phone. Susan and Eric watched while he punched in a number and then spoke to someone. "We have an injured seal down here at the institute beach. Please send a rescue team."

Mr. Wood hung up and looked at Susan. "I don't know how you spotted this creature," he said. "I'm sure it owes its life to you because you acted so quickly."

"Oh, she always acts quickly," Eric said, making a face at Susan.

"Will it be OK?" Susan asked, standing up and looking at Mr. Wood. She brushed a tear from her cheek.

"I believe it will," Mr. Wood said, patting her shoulder.

Soon, a team of marine biologists arrived in a red Jeep. They examined the seal and discovered another gash in its right side. "This little one is hurt, all right," one of them said as he scooped the seal up and placed it on a stretcher that hung from hooks in the back of the vehicle. Then the biologists said Goodbye and drove off, and Mr. Wood, Susan, and Eric made their way back to the lab.

When they entered the room, they found Aunt Sally looking at Susan's computer screen. Susan spilled the story out.

"Let's go home," Aunt Sally said. "Looks like you two have had an eventful day."

"I'm sorry I wasn't paying attention to the pictures," Susan said to Eric as they climbed into the car. "We didn't get much done today. I guess I can never be like you."

"Susan," Eric said, "you wouldn't have spotted the seal if you had been staring at the computer screen every second, like me."

"That's right," Aunt Sally said. "You can't be just like Eric."

"What would we do without you bouncing around, Susan?" Eric said, awkwardly patting her on the shoulder. "And who would have ever noticed that a log on a far-off beach was really a seal in trouble? I like you the way you are," he added, looking shy for having said so much about how he felt.

"But what's special about me?" Susan wailed.

"You're the fun-loving girl who makes our lives interesting. We don't know all you will become, but it will be amazing." Aunt Sally laughed. "And don't worry about the seal. We'll call Mr. Wood later to see how things are going."

As soon as Susan got home, she ran to her room, opened a notebook, and wrote about her adventure. She tried to capture with words the way she felt when she discovered the seal. When she finished, she read the words and felt satisfied with her work.

The next Sunday, Susan found an excuse not to join Eric at the lab. She felt sure he could get more done without her there. Feeling restless, she wandered about the house until suddenly she found herself in the doorway of Aunt Sally's office. She walked in and poked around the room until she was standing in front of a large bookcase that covered one whole wall. She scanned the titles of the first six shelves. "Every one of these books has something to do with the sea, God the Creator, or writing," she said out loud. "Aunt Sally loves to discover sea creatures, study about them, and write about what she has learned. This must be what's important to her."

On a shelf near the bottom, Susan spotted a row of books about writing. She grabbed a book that said *Creative Writing* on the spine. *I bet Aunt Sally uses these books to help her write those interesting articles. I could learn something from this book*, she thought, tucking the book under her arm.

Susan sat down on the floor so she could read the titles of the books on the bottom shelves. She moved a large queen conch shell so she could see the books at the far right end of the lowest shelf. Five brightly colored books sat in a row. *Island Adventure*, one title said. Susan picked it up and noticed the author's name, Judith Smith, written in fancy letters on the title page. The other books had the same name on their covers too. Susan didn't know a Judith Smith, but she felt drawn to the books. She read the first few paragraphs of the one she had picked up, and she found herself laughing. She decided to take the book to her room and read it. "I'll ask Aunt Sally about these later," she said to herself as she stood up.

"Susan?" Aunt Sally said, entering the office.

"Hi," Susan said, slipping *Island Adventure* behind the writing book. "I was just selecting something to read. Is that OK?"

"Certainly," Aunt Sally said, looking hard at Susan. "Are you looking for anything special?"

"Not really," she said.

Susan walked out holding the books against chest. She didn't know why she felt uncomfortable. Aunt Sally must have seen which book she had taken from the bottom shelf, from behind the seashell. Maybe she felt curious about why Susan had chosen *Island Adventure*, or perhaps she just wanted to talk about the book. *It must be a favorite of hers*, Susan thought. *But why was it hidden behind the shell?*

Susan ran to her room and plunked down onto her bed. *Island Adventure*, Susan read again. *Maybe this author had some fun experiences like I did on Eleuthera*, she thought.

Two hours passed. Susan found the book exciting and funny. She burrowed further into her quilt and continued to read.

"I'm going to get Eric at the institute," Aunt Sally called up the stairs. "Want to come along?"

"Not this time," Susan called back, hardly taking her eyes from the words on the page.

For the next two weeks, Susan spent every spare moment reading. She didn't have much time because of the SCUBA lessons, homework, and packing. Whenever Eric entered her room and found her glued to the book, she slammed it shut and tucked it under her pillow.

"What's so great about that book?" he asked one day.

"Nothing," Susan said. "It's just a story about someone's sea adventures." Susan couldn't tell Eric that she felt excited to see how the author used words to paint pictures, to describe unusual creatures, and to tell about fantastic adventures. *She just makes me want to keep reading,* Susan thought.

Eric shrugged his shoulders and said, "I came to tell you that Aunt Sally wants us to help her shop for some new SCUBA gear."

"New gear!" Susan shouted, jumping up. She laid the book on her dresser and followed Eric down the stairs. They spent the afternoon selecting the equipment they would need. They started with the BCDs. These vests held weights that would help them stay down in the water when that was what they wanted to do. The vests also had an air bladder that they could fill when they wanted to rise to the surface—something especially important if an emergency happened. They also picked out the regulators that would supply them the air they would breathe underwater, fins, masks, snorkels, knives, and dive suits. Susan chose a royal blue and black suit, and Eric picked a yellow and black one.

"The next step is to try out each piece of equipment in the pool," Aunt Sally said. "Then you'll know how each piece fits and how to operate it. I think you'll find that will make it easier for you to get through your SCUBA classes."

Susan slipped into her new BCD. "It looks great," Eric said. "These pockets are for your weights, and this is the cord you pull to drop them if you have an emergency and need to come up to the surface suddenly. Don't use this except in a big emergency," he added.

"Look," Susan said, "the air bladder is on the back."

"That's a new idea," Aunt Sally said. "My vest had air space that wrapped around me. Whenever I pumped air into it, I got a bit of a squeeze."

"This is the button you push to fill your vest," Eric said. "Or you can puff air into it through this mouthpiece." He grabbed the mouthpiece and blew, and Susan felt air enter the bladder on the back of her vest.

"This button releases the air, so you can go down," Aunt Sally said.

"I like the big zipper that closes the front," Susan said.

"They sure have improved these vests," Aunt Sally said. "I think it's time for me to purchase a new one myself."

For the next five weeks, Susan and Eric attended SCUBA class for five hours each Monday afternoon. They learned how to calculate how long they could stay down at different levels below the surface of the sea and how to descend clearing their ears. They practiced ascending safely to the surface and learned how to enter the sea from a boat by falling off backwards. Susan struggled with the math test, and Eric fumbled with his weights, but they spent a lot of time enjoying the art of being fish-like beneath the sea.

"You can't talk down there," Susan said as she broke the surface after one dive. "I saw a shark slither right beneath you, Eric. I tried to wave at you, and I even made a fist and thrust out my arm to give you the danger signal, but you didn't pay any attention."

"Wow!" Eric said, pumping extra air into his BCD to hold him up. "I couldn't see stuff on either side of me. This mask limits my view of things."

Aunt Sally, Uncle Merle, Susan, and Eric spent many afternoons checking and rechecking gear lists. They threw out some items and added new ones. By December 1, they felt ready to head to the Cayman Islands.

They flew from California to Florida, then south over Cuba, and on to Grand Cayman. "There it is," Susan shouted as they neared the island.

"It looks like a fat kidney bean," Eric said.

"You would think of food at a time like this," Susan complained, and then giggled.

"Look at the row of white that almost rings the island," Uncle Merle said, pointing out the window. "That reef system gives a lot of protection to the island during storms."

"Wow!" Eric whistled. Then he patted the camera box that lay on the seat beside him.

"I know you want to dash off to the sea the minute we land," Aunt Sally said, laughing. "But we need to go through customs, shop for groceries, and prepare our gear for tomorrow morning's dive."

"That will take forever," Eric grumbled.

"We're a professional team, and we have to act like one," Susan said, punching Eric.

As soon as the plane's engines stopped, they gathered their carry-on bags and stepped into the sunlight. Warm, moist air hit Susan's face. It felt wonderful. She saw palm trees, flowering bushes, and lots of blue sky. When they reached their cottage, they lugged their bags up a flight of stairs and into the living room, and then they headed for town to buy groceries.

When they returned to the cottage, Uncle Merle asked them to gather their gear into the living room. "We will assemble gear together," he said. "I want to know that each piece of gear is present and working well. The team is like a chain—only as strong as its weakest link. One forgotten mask, and no one dives.

"Use this list to help you get things together," he said, handing each person a piece of paper. "I covered the lists with clear plastic because I suspect we will have very few dry moments from here on."

Susan examined her BCD, reminding herself of each feature and how it worked. She slipped a two-pound net bag of lead pellets into each of the four weight pockets and set the vest aside. Next, she found her new dive bag and zipped it open. She placed her blue fins, mask, snorkel, and knife on the bottom and added a small, waterproof box containing her after-dive eardrops, a comb, and a small bag of trail mix. Then she placed her dive boots on top and zipped the bag closed. *I love those boots*, she thought. *Imagine finding ones trimmed in blue and having a picture of my favorite fish, the moorish idol, right on top.*

Susan looked over at Eric. He had his card propped up in front of him and was placing items into his yellow bag. Then everyone attached their regulators and BCDs to tanks that held three thousand pounds of compressed air. They were ready to go.

Susan decided to take a walk before settling down for the evening. She grabbed her mask and snorkel out of her dive bag and wandered out of the cottage and onto the beach. *Why did I bring this thing?* she thought, holding up her mask. Then she laughed. Aunt Sally always took her mask, even when she went to town. "I might need it for an unexpected surprise," she had said when Susan asked her why she toted it everywhere.

The sun hovered low in the tropical sky, but the air felt warm, and the water looked inviting. Susan found herself wading into the water. She knew she shouldn't swim alone. *I'll just lie here in this shallow water a few feet off shore and watch whatever fish go by,* she thought, pulling on her mask and snorkel and lying down.

She had just dropped below the surface to look at something on the bottom, when suddenly, the sky went black and the water darkened. She stared ahead. A large, flat creature with spreading black wings appeared just ahead of her. Two flat "arms" scooped water into the creature's huge mouth.

The creature stared at Susan with beady eyes, and she wanted to scream. *This monster is going to scoop me into its terrible mouth,* she thought. *No one will ever know what happened to me!* She wanted to jump up and dash for shore, but she couldn't stop staring at the creature that lay before her. *It could crush me with its wings,* she thought, *or stab me with that long, pointed, dagger tail.*

Before Susan could think of what to do, the creature turned and sailed off into the deeper sea like a seagull on an unseen current of wind. Susan stood up. The sun looked as bright as ever, and the water sparkled azure blue again. She walked out of the water and back to the cottage. *That huge creature looked so powerful,* she thought. *But it didn't hurt me. I wonder what it was.*

Susan headed for her room. She hoped no one would ask her where she'd been. She decided never to go into the water alone. *And I have to learn more about the creatures I might meet there,* she thought.

That night she felt good snuggling into her bed. She took time to read another chapter in *Island Adventure.* She liked the strong verbs the author used to show action. She decided to find time to read each day. *I wonder what it will be like out on the reef in the middle of the deep blue sea,* she wondered, and then she fell asleep.

CHAPTER 3

FIRST
DIVE

When a basketball-orange sun bounced over the horizon and into the sky, Eric yanked on Susan's ponytail. "Get up," he said. "We're going diving at Eden Rock."

Susan yawned. She looked out the window. Tiny waves rippled toward shore, and a distant line of breaks made a thin white line half a mile offshore. She leaped out of bed and grabbed her swimsuit.

As soon as they ate breakfast, they loaded equipment into the station wagon and jumped in. Uncle Merle backed out onto the road, and they sped away.

"Watch out!" Susan screamed as she threw one arm up in front of her face. "You're driving on the wrong side of the road!"

Susan's sudden outburst surprised Uncle Merle, and he jerked the steering wheel to the left for an instant. Then he laughed, and Aunt Sally and Eric laughed too. Susan looked at them, a frown creasing her forehead.

"You aren't about to die," Eric said. "In the Cayman Islands, people are supposed to drive on the left side of the road."

"Oh!" Susan said. "I forgot we were in a different country."

"Lots of things will seem strange," Aunt Sally said. "Check with me before you spend your money. There's about a twenty percent difference between Cayman Islands dollars and American dollars." Aunt Sally handed Susan and Eric a Cayman Islands ten-dollar bill to look at.

"Wow," Susan said. "It says, 'Cayman Islands Monetary Authority.' There's even a picture of the queen on it. And coral, palm trees, and a treasure chest."

They drove along a two-lane road that hugged the coast. Some of the island was edged in sand, and some ended abruptly in jagged, low coral cliffs.

"Look at that house!" Eric said. "The roof is gone, and so are the windows. And every tree in the yard has fallen over."

"It looks like the sea reached in, yanked them up, and threw them down," Susan said.

"That's hurricane damage," Uncle Merle said. "The wind drove water over parts of the island, smashing out windows, flipping cars over, and uprooting trees. Of course, the houses nearest the coast got the most damage."

"I think we'll discover some major reef destruction," Aunt Sally said. "I hate to see that."

Uncle Merle pulled off the road and parked next to a building just a few feet back from the sea. "Eden Rock," a sign said.

Susan and Eric jumped out. They walked around, looking at the row of picnic tables with awnings, an outside shower, and a large concrete box full of water. These sat on a concrete slab on top of a cliff that jutted into the sea.

"How do we get into the water?" Susan asked, looking out over the azure sea.

"Just climb down this ladder," Eric said, pointing to a stainless steel ladder that hugged the slab and plunged down into the water.

"That looks steep," Susan groaned.

"Nice setup," Uncle Merle said, coming up behind the twins who stared down at the ladder. "You go down backwards and carry your fins with their straps looped over your arms," he said. "It's really easy. I'll show you how."

"The water is shallow here," Eric said. "I think we can get our fins on without too much trouble."

"Let's go see how Aunt Sally is doing," Uncle Merle said. "She may have some difficulty renting the large number of tanks we'll need."

Aunt Sally was talking with a woman with an Australian accent, short curly hair, and a big smile. "My name is Dorothy," the woman was saying. "The institute contacted me about your project. They purchased twenty tanks for your use. You can fill them here as often as you need to. We're glad to assist you any way we can."

Aunt Sally smiled. "Mr. Wood has taken care of everything," she said to Uncle Merle when he and the twins arrived at the shop door.

"Hi, kids," Dorothy said. "I hear you'll be doing some serious diving for the next few weeks."

"That's right," the twins said at the same time.

"We want to begin here on the west side," Aunt Sally said. "This is where the hurricane hit the hardest."

"Good idea," Dorothy said. "This reef consists of many forty- to sixty-foot pillars of coral with sand between. It's easy to inspect each pillar, determine the damage, and count species."

"Thank you for your help," Aunt Sally said as they left the shop and headed toward their car.

"Let's suit up," Uncle Merle said.

Susan struggled into her dive suit. It stuck to her skin, and she had to tug at it. Then she put on her boots and BCD. She started to feel hot beneath the tropical sun. Perspiration ran down her face. It tasted salty.

"Here," Uncle Merle said, dumping a bottle of water over her head.

"Stop!" Susan screamed. Then she grinned and said, "No, don't stop. That feels good."

Eric laughed. "Give me a cool-down too," he said.

"You'll learn to suit up a bit faster as we go along," Aunt Sally said. "It isn't good to get overheated."

Uncle Merle lifted Susan's air tank and helped her get it on her back. It felt heavy. Then she hung her mask and fins over her arms as Eric had suggested, and she walked, hunched over, to the ladder. Aunt Sally steadied her with her hand and said, "At least we don't have to wear a weight belt. The weights just fit into our vest pockets. I've always hated that weight belt around my waist."

"You put defogger drops into your masks, didn't you?" Uncle Merle asked.

"Yes," Susan and Eric chorused.

Uncle Merle opened the air valve on each of their air tanks, checked their gear, and demonstrated how to back down the ladder. "I'll be right here. This gets easier and easier, and remember, you'll be able to get near what you see," he said,

Susan reviewed the tasks needed to get ready for and complete each dive. It seemed so demanding and complex. Suddenly, she felt scared. She wondered if they would remember all the rules about safe diving. SCUBA diving seemed like a lot of work just to swim beside a fish for a few minutes. *I don't think I can do this*, she thought.

Then she saw Eric grab his camera. A big smile spread across his face as he looked out over the water. *I'll just take it one step at a time*, she thought. *If I think about the whole process at once, I might give up. I can do one step at a time. Anyway, this is what it takes to become a diver. I can do this.*

Eric followed Susan, and Aunt Sally followed both of them into the cooling sea. They sat in the water, facing each other, wiggled into their fins, grasped the mouthpiece that delivered the life-giving air, and adjusted their masks. Then Susan kicked her fins and trailed the others as they left the land behind them.

When the water got deeper, she released the air in her vest so she could sink. She pinched her nose and blew out to clear her ears. She could see the sand below her. When she neared the bottom, she hovered three feet above it, lay on her stomach like Uncle Merle, and faced the outer reef area. She was diving.

They finned slowly along, just above the sea floor. Soon, tall pillars of coral appeared in the distance. They looked gray and ghostly, like stubby trees in a forest. But as she neared one, she saw that colorful algae, sea fans, and sponges clung to every inch of the pillar. And small fish flitted around and around, poked from crevices, or just lay still next to the coral.

Susan felt like a stranger in a fascinating alien world. She swallowed an urge to shout and held herself back from dashing off in every direction at once. She watched Eric and Uncle Merle stop and focus their cameras on a tiny fairy basslet. Its yellow and purple scales flashed under the stream of light from Eric's camera lights.

Susan noticed a stingray off to her right. She tapped Eric on the arm and pointed to the ray. Eric and Uncle Merle moved slowly after it. Aunt Sally stared at the coral and wrote something on her dive slate. She shook her head and frowned. Susan made a mental note to ask her what was wrong when they surfaced after the dive.

Susan tried to stay still and take deep, regular breaths. Suddenly, she spotted a big tiger grouper and kicked her fins, following it around the backside of the coral pillar. When she came back to Eric and Uncle Merle, Aunt Sally held her dive slate up close to Susan's face. SLOW DOWN, the slate said.

Minutes later, a flash of action caught Susan's eye. She turned around and discovered a school of blue tangs sweeping around a pillar close by. She swam after them and discovered that a cave ran right through the coral pillar. She could see the far end because light from the surface shone into it. She glanced around. Aunt Sally, Uncle Merle, and Eric looked busy taking notes and pictures. No one was looking at her. Susan couldn't resist swimming through the cave. *I'll be in and out in seconds*, she told herself.

The cave looked dark, and its walls were bare. No fish swam around inside of it. Susan felt relieved when she reached the far end and burst into the light.

A large queen conch sat on the sand just beyond her. It had created a long, curling trail as it had slithered over the sand. Susan let a bit of air out of her BCD and dropped to the sand. She picked up the shell, running her fingers over the smooth surface. Instantly a tiny fish darted out, fleeing to the cover of a rocky ledge nearby. Susan placed the shell back onto the sand. In a moment, the little fish returned to its hiding place under the flat lip of the shell. Susan smiled. Two thin, round antennae stuck out of the shell. There was a tiny eye at the end of each one. *That creature is a mollusk,* Susan thought. She remembered seeing them in many shells in the Bahamas.

Suddenly, Susan realized she was alone. She whirled in a complete circle. The distant coral pillars stared at her, gray and ghostly. She wanted to see her dive partners right now. Her heart beat like waves smashing against rocks offshore. She didn't want to go around the pillar into strange territory nor back through the cave. Then she got an idea. *I'll just go up and over the pillar*, she thought. *I know they're on the other side.* She ascended slowly, swam across the pillar, and looked down.

She saw three streams of bubbles flowing toward the surface. They looked beautiful to her. As each bubble rose toward the surface, it became bigger and bigger. She hung suspended and watched as Uncle Merle turned from the fish that floated in front of his camera and looked around. *They don't see me,* she thought. *Why don't they look up?*

Susan dropped down, concentrating on moving slowly and clearing her ears. She dropped right into the middle of the others. They jerked back and stared at her. She wanted to say, "Sorry I scared you," but she couldn't. She thought she might hear about this incident later.

Susan signaled for the others to follow her, and then she swam to the entrance of the cave. She watched Eric slither through the cave after Aunt Sally and Uncle Merle. His eyes widened, and he waved to her as he emerged. He picked up the queen conch after Susan nudged him toward it. The tiny fish took off for a new hiding place. Susan showed them that it would come right back when it felt the coast was clear. Aunt Sally looked pleased with Susan and gave her the OK signal.

Far too soon, Uncle Merle put his hands flat, one ahead of the other, and made a forward movement with both of them Susan knew that gesture to be the "follow me" signal and that it was time to head for shore. They swam along just above the upward slope of the sea floor, getting closer to the surface each minute. Susan watched her gauges. Soon she popped through the surface, pumped air into her vest, and floated to the ladder, kicking her fins.

"Wow," Susan shouted, not waiting to get out of the water to express her excitement. "That was amazing!"

"What's amazing is the way you flitted around out there," Eric said. "Then you disappeared altogether."

"Well, you just stayed in one place and stared at the coral," Susan shot back, struggling up the ladder.

"Check your gauges," Eric complained. "I bet you used twice as much air as the rest of us."

"You two definitely have different dive styles," Aunt Sally said, removing her vest and dumping it into the rinse tank.

"Of course, we probably wouldn't have discovered the cave if Susan hadn't been doing her usual exploring," Uncle Merle added.

When they had packed up their gear and were headed home, Aunt Sally said, "It's all right to dive differently, but there have to be parameters."

"Parameters?" Susan said.

"Guidelines," Aunt Sally said. "First, stay with your dive partner. Second, go slowly. Move about with steady, relaxed motions. You will use less air this way and not have to cut your dive short."

Eric made a face at Susan.

"Third, always let your dive partner know what you're doing before you do it," Aunt Sally said, looking at Susan. "And you should work with your dive partner to include activities both of you want to do so that everyone has a good dive. That's why it's a good idea to agree on a plan for your dive before you do it."

"Maybe I could spend some of my time exploring," Eric said. "I sure liked that cave."

Aunt Sally and Uncle Merle smiled at each other. "Now you're acting like reef creatures," Aunt Sally said.

"I know what you mean," Susan said. "They all live in symbiotic relationships."

"What kind of relationship?" Eric asked

"It means that they get along," Susan said.

"*Symbiosis* is a word that describes cooperation between different kinds of creatures," Uncle Merle said.

"Like the queen conch and the conch fish," Susan said. "The helpless little fish gets free protection from the heavy edge of the shell. But what does the queen conch get from the conch fish?"

"No one knows that yet," Aunt Sally said. "In some symbiotic relationships, both partners benefit. Scientists call that mutualism. In commensual symbiosis, one partner receives some kind of benefit while the other partner isn't helped—but it doesn't get injured either."

"And some creatures actually hurt their host in some way. In that case, the partner is called a parasite," Uncle Merle said.

"Eric, let's be an example of mutualism," Susan said laughing. "I'll find stuff, and you snag a picture."

"These knobby-heads will make a good team yet," Uncle Merle said, smiling at Aunt Sally.

"Are you saying we can keep them both?" Aunt Sally teased.

Then Susan asked, "Why did you frown so much when you took notes down there?"

"I saw a lot of damaged coral. In fact, the whole area looked like an old, barren reef. I didn't see even one sea fan and only a few soft corals."

"If that was a damaged reef, just think of how a healthy one would look," Susan said.

When they arrived back at the cottage, Aunt Sally suggested, "Before we hit the showers, let's clean and reorganize our gear so it's ready for tomorrow. After that we can have a hot supper and talk about our experiences on the reef."

"Uncle Merle," Susan said when she had finally completed her tasks and pulled a chair up to the supper table. "I think I understand something new because of that dive today."

"What's that?" Uncle Merle said.

"God invented church," Susan said.

"Of course He did," Eric interrupted.

"I mean for a special reason," Susan said, looking serious. "Every member is different, but each one is important. That's what makes the family of God interesting."

"And powerful," Uncle Merle said, handing Eric the bowl of mashed potatoes for the third time.

"Powerful?" Eric said. "I like that idea."

"Certainly," Aunt Sally said. "The very fact that each member is different helps the whole church function with more power and joy."

"God certainly has great ideas," Uncle Merle said. "He gives each person a gift or ability and helps them each to develop and use their gifts."

"When do you get these gifts?" Susan asked, leaning toward Uncle Merle and studying his face. "I want them."

"God will help you discover and use your natural gifts and abilities. He also gives gifts to fit a special need. Sometimes we learn about our gifts gradually, but God has promised that, at your baptism, when you make that total commitment, He will open your mind to new ideas and ways to use these gifts."

Susan thought about what Uncle Merle said. She remembered that she and Eric had decided to be baptized and join God's family several months ago but hadn't yet acted on the idea. Suddenly, she really wanted to know what God had in mind for her.

"—and I feel ready to go ahead with my plan to be baptized," Eric was saying. "What about you, Susan?"

"Yes," Susan blurted. "I'm ready. And I want to do it right here in the surf."

"There isn't any reason for delay," Uncle Merle said. "You both made your decision to follow Jesus before we went to Eleuthera Island last summer, and you've had your baptismal classes. I'll call Pastor McDonald and arrange things."

The next Sabbath, after the sermon, Susan and Eric stood in the azure blue water just offshore. The local church members gathered around them, standing in the dry sand. Susan looked up at the little church. She was in a strange country, yet she would be part of these people and this family—God's family.

The pastor led the twins into the water. Susan's robe swirled around her in the ebb and flow of the tiny wavelets. A trail of white clouds danced across the sky, pushed by the wind. Pastor McDonald prayed. "We are full of joy today that these two young people have chosen to become part of Your family, dear God. Bless them with an understanding of the plan You have for their lives, and give them gifts that will help them serve You in some special way. Amen." Then the people sang as he plunged Susan beneath the water.

As she came up into the sunlight, she thought about God washing away her sins, and she remembered that she was rising to a new, special life of service for her heavenly Father. She would watch, really watch, to see what God might want to give her as gifts so she could be part of His plan to help people know Him and live forever.

She smiled to herself and sighed. *I don't have to be like Eric or anyone else; I can be myself,* she thought. *I'm important to God. He'll show me how to use my personality and my abilities to serve Him.* She felt wonderful.

"Now you're part of the family," Pastor McDonald said, wiping her face and giving her a hug. Susan stood still as Eric disappeared beneath the water. He came up with a big smile on his face. "Welcome to the family, son," Pastor McDonald said.

Susan and Eric turned toward shore, and Susan looked up. Aunt Sally and Uncle Merle were running toward them. Aunt Sally ran right into the water and grabbed them both. "Your shoes!" Uncle Merle yelled. "Take off your shoes." But it was too late; Aunt Sally kept coming. "I'm so happy," she said over and over. "I'm just so happy."

Mrs. McDonald invited them to a special dinner to celebrate the day. "This food is so delicious," Susan said. "I don't know what it is, but I like it." Everyone laughed. Susan noticed that the McDonalds laughed a lot. She liked them immediately. Susan and Eric met several of the island young people and talked about their reef project.

The next day they dived at Eden Rock again. Susan didn't try to dash off in every direction; she hung in front of the coral pillars, staring. She asked herself three questions. What is each creature doing? What shape, color, or parts do they have that enable them to do what they do? How do they work together?

She saw a parrotfish hanging just above an outcropping of lettuce coral, its mouth agape and its fins extended from its plump, colorful body. Six tiny, slender, yellow-striped cleaner gobies swarmed over it and into its mouth. Susan stared. *Mutualism,* she thought. The parrotfish gets parasites cleaned off its body, and the cleaner gobies get a free meal.

Suddenly, she got an idea. She removed the glove from her right hand and moved it toward the fish. The parrot-fish sped away. Susan stayed motionless, hand extended. In a few minutes, the tiny gobies swarmed over her palm. She felt tiny pinching sensations as they searched the surface of her hand for edibles. Susan laughed, and a burst of bubbles frightened off the fish.

When they finished the dive, Susan blurted out her story. "I know all about it," Eric said. "I was right behind you, taking pictures."

"Thanks, Eric," Susan said, wadding up her beach towel as a pillow and leaning against it.

"The good thing about pictures is that you can relive your experience later," Eric said. But Susan didn't hear him. She had fallen asleep, still smiling.

CHAPTER 4

THE SURPRISE AT BABYLON REEF

"Are you telling me that the boat won't be ready for two days or more?" Aunt Sally asked. Then she groaned and flopped down into a chair. Susan could see her knuckles turn white as she grasped the phone. "But as it is, we have only three weeks to complete the project," she said. "We can't spare two days." Then she mumbled, "Goodbye," and dropped the phone onto her lap.

"What's the matter, Sally?" Uncle Merle asked.

"The boat is broken," Susan blurted.

"Now don't worry—we'll think of something," Uncle Merle soothed.

"What's going on?" Eric said, coming into the room.

"We can't dive today," Susan said. "Something is wrong with the boat."

"Oh no," Eric complained.

"Sally, I know this isn't the kind of surprise you want, but I have an idea," Uncle Merle said, pacing the room. "Didn't you say that your friends Clyde and Reggie did a lot of shore diving on the part of the island called the East End?"

"Yes. They spent a month diving and didn't use a boat once. They swam out from shore, descended down to the shallow reef, and sometimes continued out over the wall. They told me the reef looked healthy and the photographic opportunities were fantastic," she said.

"Let's do that," Susan said, her eyes lighting up.

"Wait a minute, all of you," Aunt Sally said. "The shallow reef is almost a quarter mile offshore."

"I know, Sally," Uncle Merle said. "But I think these knobby-heads could handle it. We could go down one of the buoy lines and spend our time exploring the shallow reef. I believe it begins at a depth of about twenty-five feet."

Aunt Sally sat silent for a long moment. "I don't think Susan and Eric are ready for the deeper reef nor for the wall," she said. "I'm sure they could handle the shallow reef. But it is a long swim," she added, looking at the twins.

"We can do it," Eric said.

"I believe they can," Uncle Merle said. "This way you can get the data you need—"

"And Eric can get his pictures," Susan said. "Please?"

"OK. We'll give it a try," Aunt Sally said.

"Good!" Uncle Merle said. "Sit down, Susan and Eric. I want to go over our dive plan in detail. First, we'll inflate our BCDs and lie on our backs, kicking our fins slowly, and move together toward the reef. I'll check our progress from time to time. We'll pass over sand, then scattered corals, and finally reach the reef. I think it will take about a half hour. I'll try to find a buoy on a line. If I find one, we can descend using it to help orient us and to give us more control in clearing our ears. If I can't find a buoy, we'll face each other and go down together feet first."

"I'm still a bit uncomfortable about this plan," Aunt Sally said. "If we meet up with any surprises, anything we aren't expecting, we'll return to shore immediately."

"OK," the twins chorused.

They collected their gear, stashed it in the car, and headed down the Queens Highway, which hugged the coast. Susan stared at the ocean, but she couldn't see the white line of breakers that marks most reefs.

"Uncle Merle," she asked. "Where's the reef? I can't see any breakers."

"Good question, Susan. Because the top of Babylon Reef is more than twenty-five feet beneath the surface, the waves don't crash on it," Uncle Merle said. "Some small white buoys mark the edge of the reef."

"It must be a long ways out there. I can't see any buoys," Susan said.

Uncle Merle parked in a short pullout space just above a low, sloping dune. "Suit up. Let's see how it goes. If we don't reach Babylon Reef, we can enjoy the patchy reef just off shore."

Eric lugged his bag out of the car and set it on a patch of grass. He wiggled into his suit, but Susan noticed that he kept glancing out at the sea. She got her suit on as fast as she could to avoid overheating. *It sure is a long way out to that buoy*, she thought. *I wish we had a boat.* She heard Uncle Merle whistling as he tugged on his dive suit. He carried the tanks down to the edge of the water. Susan, Aunt Sally, and Eric hauled their gear down, attached the vests to the tanks, and hooked up all the hoses. Uncle Merle helped Susan make her way across the sand and over the rocks that hugged the shore. Then he lifted her vest and tank onto her back. She waited while the others got their gear on too.

When all of them were ready, Uncle Merle told them to walk out until they got into shoulder-deep water, put on their fins, and lie on their backs. "Be sure to put enough air in your BCD to keep you comfortably afloat. You can breathe through your snorkel as we float along, but you don't need to. I think using one makes breathing a lot of work," he said.

The four divers moved farther and farther from shore. "This isn't bad," Eric said, looking around.

"I can't help but wonder what's swimming beneath us," Susan said.

Uncle Merle shoved his mask on, turned to his side, and looked down. "The water is empty; there's only white sand below," he said when he rolled onto his back again.

As Uncle Merle guided them toward the buoy, they talked about what they might see on the reef and the data Aunt Sally needed to get. Uncle Merle turned over again, and then he jerked his head out of the water. "Look down!" he shouted.

Everyone put on their masks and turned to face the sea floor. Susan could see beautiful patches of reef scattered over the sand. Fish swirled around the corals, darting in and out. She spotted a long, gray shape farther out. "It's the big reef," she sputtered when she turned on her back again. "We're almost there."

In another ten minutes, they reached a buoy. Susan grabbed the rope that disappeared into the depth. Somehow, touching it soothed her. When Aunt Sally signaled for them to descend, Susan clung with one hand to the line and released all the air from her BCD. Then she let herself slip deeper and deeper, clearing her ears every few seconds. Colored fish swam past her, and she had to swallow a laugh that tried to burst out. She looked over to see Aunt Sally and Uncle Merle going down feet first. They didn't cling to the rope. Eric let go from time to time and then reached out to slow his descent. Susan thought, *Soon Eric and I will be able to descend as easily as Aunt Sally and Uncle Merle did.*

When they all reached the reef, they leveled off and started to explore. Susan saw a spotted eel sticking its head out of a small crevice. She motioned to Eric, who swam over and pointed his camera at it. Susan glanced around. Purple sea fans, soft corals, and tube sponges swayed in the gentle current. She didn't know which way to explore first. She decided to check her gauges. They said that she had three thousand pounds of air and that she was thirty feet below the surface.

Creatures and plants lived on every square inch of the reef. They formed a wild kaleidoscope of colors, patterns, shapes, and textures. Joy surged up inside Susan and tried to burst out of her. She wanted to talk to Eric, but, of course, she couldn't.

She turned on her side and faced the reef, staring at all the small bits of color. Then she saw a patch of gray. It didn't look like it belonged on the reef. She moved closer to check it out. When she did, she spotted more gray areas behind large coral formations and sea fans that formed a kind of holey cave. *What could be big and gray and smooth?* she wondered. She motioned for Eric to come.

When he drew closer, the gray moved slightly. Eric froze. Then he looked at Susan, eyes wide. She looked at the gray again and gulped. Suddenly, she saw a big black, beady eye. "It's a shark," she screamed at Eric. She knew that only sharks had eyes like that. She had seen them on the shark that she and Aunt Sally had almost swum into in the canal on Eleuthera Island.

Susan gasped. The shark looked like it was asleep. *What if it wakes up?* she thought. She and Eric grabbed at the water to turn themselves. They kicked their fins and tried to back away, but they rammed into Uncle Merle and Aunt Sally. Susan screamed, and her regulator popped out of her mouth. Eric grabbed it and jammed it back in before she could think what to do. She remembered to punch the purge button, and a burst of air cleared all the water out of her mouth. She sucked in a gulp of air. Then Aunt Sally placed a hand on her shoulder, scribbled something on the dive slate, and held it up. "It's OK," the words said. "Stay still a moment."

"Stay still?" Susan shouted into her mouthpiece. "What if that shark wakes up?"

Of course, no one understood her garbled words. They all stared at the shark and hung silently in the water. Then Uncle Merle nudged Eric, and they moved toward the shark, so Susan followed. Eric found another hole in the "cave," and he and Uncle Merle peered in. Susan and Aunt Sally looked over their shoulders. The size of the dorsal fins and tail told them that this was a very big shark. Eric took pictures as fast as he could. He started to move even closer, but Uncle Merle motioned for them to go on. Susan heaved a sigh of relief. She had imagined that every flash of the camera's strobe would be the one to arouse the sleeping shark. She groaned. *I have no boat to flee into,* she thought.

Aunt Sally swam up to Susan and smiled. She gave the dive sign for "follow me," but Susan didn't need a sign; she practically clung to Aunt Sally. *What other creatures live out here that I can't swim away from?* she wondered, her heart banging like the pounding of a tropical downpour. *The sea is full of surprises.*

Soon they spotted a small stingray and stopped to take pictures. The shark seemed forgotten. They swam all over the shallow reef, pausing for pictures so often that Susan had time to take short trips to snoop into holes and around pillars of coral. Finally, they moved toward the edge of the reef that faced shore. Uncle Merle signaled for them to gather at the anchor line. Susan felt glad to see the line. It helped her figure out where she was and where the shore was. *I'm learning*, she thought to herself.

Uncle Merle signaled them to follow him. He didn't ascend to the surface. Instead, he headed toward shore, swimming just above the sandy bottom. Susan watched as the reef receded behind them. She stopped for a moment at several patches of coral and then moved over the sandy plain that spread out before her like a miniature desert.

Susan saw a peacock flounder slither into a hiding place beneath the sand, and she watched a rainbow parrotfish grasp a chunk of coral and grind it up with strong teeth. Every creature did something different, and none of them seemed confused about what they were supposed to do. They didn't look scared either. *That's what I want, dear Jesus,* she prayed. *I want to be myself and to learn what my special purpose for living is. And I don't want to be scared about what surprises lie ahead. Please help me.*

Susan looked at her gauges. By following the sea floor toward shore, they had moved from thirty feet deep to only ten feet. She hadn't minded the long journey toward shore; she liked seeing the sea floor change. She smiled in spite of herself.

"Ascend," Uncle Merle said by pointing upward with his thumb. Susan puffed a bit of air into her BCD by pushing a special button, and she burst through the surface of the water, joining the others. Then they lay on their backs and kicked.

As they moved along, Eric said, "Every corner of the reef is full of surprises."

"Yeah, like sharks," Susan replied.

Everyone laughed.

"A nurse shark won't hurt you," Eric said, "probably."

"It sure did surprise me though," Susan said.

"I think that's one of the reasons I like diving," Aunt Sally said. "I never know what I'll see on a reef. And Babylon Reef is a healthy reef bursting with life."

"Are we going back?" Eric asked, looking at his camera.

"I'm not sure," Uncle Merle said, looking at Aunt Sally and Susan.

"I liked the anchor line," Susan said, changing the subject and trying not to think about the shark anymore. "It made me feel safer in that big, open ocean."

Aunt Sally laughed. "That's what an anchor line does. It tells you where the reef is and helps you feel in control as you ascend and descend."

"Boats have to tie to that buoy so they won't drop an anchor onto the reef and damage it," Eric said. "That's true. I read that in the dive manual," he said when Susan looked at him with a frown.

The sun shone down on them, and the gentle sea swells passed by one after another as they paddled toward the shore.

"I learned something," Susan said, kicking her fins in rhythm with the others.

"You learned that a nurse shark doesn't mind having its picture taken when it's asleep," Eric said.

"I did not. Anyway, how do you know that?" Susan objected.

"It didn't wake up and eat you, did it?" Eric said, laughing.

Susan reached her finned foot out and smacked his leg. "Hey!" Eric shouted.

"What did you learn?" Aunt Sally asked.

"I learned that I really want to know where that anchor line is. It feels good to be anchored to something you can depend on."

"That's like knowing that God loves me," Eric said.

"Of course," Susan said. "Knowing that God loves me makes me feel safe. But that isn't all." Susan kicked a few more times before she continued. "You can count on the anchor line. If you got caught in a current, you could hang on until help came. It's something to attach your boat to so it won't drift off when you're diving."

"And it helps you know where you are in relation to the shore," Eric said.

"Go on," Aunt Sally encouraged, removing her mask and snorkel and hanging them over one arm. She wiped water from her face.

"I think God is like an anchor. He shows people where He wants them to be and what He wants them to do. They feel anchored that way. Nothing can pull them off in some other direction," Susan said.

"I'm anchored," Eric said.

"I know," Susan said. "You know what your special gift is—at least part of it. That's why you don't let anything pull you off in some other direction—not even baseball."

Eric stared at Susan. Then he smiled.

"But when you don't know, you feel like you're adrift in a great big ocean full of scary creatures," Susan said, looking away.

"Do you feel like that?" Eric asked, moving closer to Susan.

"Sometimes," Susan said. "I just wish I could figure things out."

"That's what you're doing right now," Aunt Sally said. "You have this time to study, to try new things, to talk to others who have it figured out, and to pray."

"You can bet that God is very interested in helping you find your anchor," Uncle Merle said. "Hey, we're in shallow water. You can take off your fins and walk in from here."

They staggered out of the water and up the hill to the car.

"Maybe it's like a treasure hunt," Eric said, pulling his dive suit off and draping it over the car door. "You know you're looking for something important, so even if you don't find it right away, you keep searching, even if you get scared by a few surprises."

"Did it work like that for you, Aunt Sally?" Susan asked. "How did you know you should become a writer and public speaker?"

"I didn't know right away," she said. "To be honest, I didn't understand the principle of spiritual gifts as I do now. I studied nursing because I liked helping people and that's what most of my friends were doing. I wish I had spent some serious time thinking about who God made me to be and how I could serve Him best. I guess I did what people expected me to do. Later, when I turned to God for help in deciding what to do with the rest of my life, He showed me that I could put words together like puzzle pieces to build a story."

Aunt Sally continued, "Someone asked me to come and speak to their women's group, and I discovered that I loved it. I used my adventures with the sea creatures to illustrate my ideas. People really listened. They felt encouraged and excited. It was like a miracle!" Aunt Sally's face lighted up as she spoke. "I learned to discover wonderful lessons in nature and in God's Word. Then I wanted to share what I learned with others. That's what I love doing, and it fits my personality," she said, her face glowing.

"God is so wonderful," Uncle Merle said, smiling at Aunt Sally. He placed a towel on the car seat and eased into the car.

"You could develop a strategy," Eric suggested, plopping onto the backseat. "I have one for getting the right shot. First, I make sure my camera is in good working order. Then, I go where the action is, and I send Susan off to find stuff."

"Yeah," Susan said, yanking Eric's wet hair. "And if I don't get eaten by the creature, you come take a picture of it."

"That's my strategy," Eric said, fending off Susan's punches.

"God has a strategy, too. He plants dreams in your heart, and He helps you reach for those dreams," Uncle Merle said. "But it doesn't happen overnight," he added.

"Neither does becoming a good diver," Aunt Sally said. "You learn more on every dive, and one day you realize you aren't paying so much attention to your gear. Instead, you're focusing on the reef."

"You mean your mask doesn't leak every other minute," Uncle Merle said.

"And you don't panic when you get surprised," Eric said, looking at Susan.

Aunt Sally laughed and then she said, "That's what I mean. The whole process takes time."

"I guess you're right," Susan said. "I'll have to keep on looking."

"You sure better," Eric urged, "or my pictures will become boring."

"I'm not talking about looking for sea creatures," Susan said, frowning. "I mean I have to keep searching for my special gifts."

"I know," Eric said, reaching over and giving Susan an

awkward pat on the shoulder. "Don't be in such a hurry. You'll figure it out."

Susan was silent as they drove toward their cottage. She looked out over the blue waters where they'd been diving. Now that she was on dry land, she was safe from surprises she didn't like. But she wouldn't see any wonderful things unless she ventured out into the sea. Surprises and all, Susan wanted to look and keep looking. She decided to live the same way. She would get out there and enjoy the adventure of living, including unexpected surprises. *And I'm going to trust in Jesus, the Anchor Line,* she thought.

"We're going out again tomorrow, aren't we?" Susan asked suddenly.

"We sure are," Uncle Merle said, casting Aunt Sally a big grin. "But right now I have a special surprise. Get your gear rinsed—picnic on the beach in thirty minutes!" he said, parking the car near the cottage.

Susan and Eric leaped out of the car, grabbed their dive bags, and raced for the back door. "I'll bring in the tanks," Uncle Merle called after them, but they had disappeared into the house.

CHAPTER 5

HIDDEN TREASURE

Susan snuggled into her quilt and grabbed the book *Island Adventure* from its hiding place beneath her pillow. She heard Eric in the next room settling in front of the computer. She smiled. Aunt Sally and Uncle Merle were off to town on business, and she and Eric had a whole afternoon to do as they pleased. She knew Eric would be glad to spend the next five hours working on the pictures he had stored on his memory card. *Right now, I'll be glad to lose myself in this story,* she thought. *I just love the way the author paints pictures with words.*

Susan read three chapters before she glanced up. The tropical sun had slid across the sky and started down toward the horizon. It sent yellow beams dancing on the azure water. She could see the thin line of breakers far offshore. *I wonder what's between shore and that reef,* she thought, stuffing the book behind a pillow.

"Eric," Susan called, "let's go snorkeling. The tide is out. Aunt Sally said that the lagoon is shallow right up to the reef. She said we could do some exploring if we wanted to."

"No," Eric called back. "I still have a lot to do in here."

"Please, Eric," Susan begged, walking into his room. "You know I shouldn't go into the water by myself."

"Well, OK," Eric said, stretching but not looking away from a picture of a moray eel on the screen.

Susan waited until he finally shut down the computer. Then they grabbed their snorkel gear and cameras and headed off across the white sand to the edge of the sea. "I bet we won't see anything but sand," Eric complained.

"There has to be something. Let's swim out to those rocks," Susan said, pointing to a cluster of rocks breaking the surface a hundred yards from shore. "Don't fish usually cluster around rocks?"

"Of course they do," Eric said, making some adjustments on his camera and wading into the sea. Susan followed. She clung to her camera as she struggled through the small line of waves and into deeper water.

They swam along over barren white sand. Small rocks covered by sand and silt lay here and there, and a few fish darted past. Eric stuck his head out of the water and noted the position of the rocks. Then he signaled for Susan to change direction a bit. Soon they spotted the gray outline of the rocks just beyond. A school of blue tangs swirled around them and then jetted off toward the reef. Lobsters peeked from crevices, twitching their antennae.

Eric and Susan circled the large patch of boulders. They chased fish, took pictures, and laughed. Anytime they wanted to rest, they just stood up in the shallow water. Before long, they had made their way to the shoreward side of the reef.

"Why, it's all dead!" Susan shouted, spitting out her snorkel and standing up.

"Sure doesn't look like Babylon Reef," Eric said.

"I know what happened," Susan said. "The hurricane blasted through here. It's so shallow that everything was blown away. The reef looks like the skeleton of a giant lizard lying here. At least this side of it does."

"Well, there isn't any point in staying here. I don't see a living thing other than the few fish that go by now and again."

"Let's rest a minute," Susan said, sitting down on a flat rock and looking toward shore. She watched children playing in the sand and people snorkeling in the shallow water. "We're a long way from shore."

"Wow!" Eric said, plopping down beside her. "It's so shallow that I didn't realize we'd come so far. Too bad there isn't anything out here."

"Just a bunch of small rocks," Susan said, picking one up. The layer of silt and sand that covered the rock slid off and clouded up the water. In a moment, the gentle current cleared the water. "Yowee!" Susan screamed, lifting her feet from the water and dropping the rock. "What was that?"

"I'm sure it's nothing," Eric said, standing up on the rock and looking into the water.

"But I saw something," Susan insisted. "It looked black and skinny. I think it went under that other rock."

Eric pushed his mask in place and jammed his snorkel into his mouth. He lay down in the water and gently lifted the rock. Two hairy creatures dashed out. In less than two seconds, they squeezed themselves under a nearby rock.

"Brittle stars," Eric shouted, lifting his head out of the water. "Get in here."

Susan put her mask and snorkel in place, lowered herself into the water, and stared. Eric overturned another rock. A brittle star and two crabs toting shells on their backs scampered away. Eric laid the rock down and took aim. But by the time he had the camera ready, the creatures had hidden themselves away again.

Eric and Susan stood up. "Fantastic!" Eric said. "But if we're going to get any good shots, we'll have to work as a team."

"What do you want me to do?" Susan asked.

"I'll focus on a particular area and then I'll signal you. Lift the rock slowly so the silt won't fly up and cloud the water. I'll squeeze off some shots. Later, we can change places so you can take some pictures too."

They floated in the water. Susan noticed that hundreds of small rocks, frosted by white silt, lay scattered up against the front of the dead reef. She could hear waves beating against the side of the reef facing the outer sea, a good distance away.

Eric selected a flat rock and floated in the water in front of it, resting his camera on the sand. Susan pressed her fingers under the edge of the rock and lifted it. Two black, hairy brittle stars with penny-sized, octagon-shaped bodies and five long, twitching legs darted right toward Eric. One squeezed under his camera.

"Whoa!" Eric shouted, leaping to his feet. The brittle stars scattered and found shelter in a crevice.

"What?" Susan shrieked, losing her snorkel. Water poured into her mask. "What happened?" she asked, standing up beside Eric and dumping the water from her mask. "Did you get the picture?"

"I think so, but I'm not sure. That thing tried to crawl under my camera."

Susan laughed. "This isn't going to be as easy as we thought," she said, adjusting her mask. "When I lift the rock this time, you start clicking right away. You're bound to get something."

The next time Susan lifted a rock, she couldn't resist the impulse to touch the brittle star. She slid her hand under the sand and lifted it up. For one moment, the black, hairy creature sat on her hand. She gulped as hundreds of black hairs brushed against her skin. Suddenly, the brittle star climbed off her hand, landed on the sand, and hurried away, looking for the nearest hiding place.

For more than three hours, Susan and Eric turned the rocks, splashing and screaming and clicking their cameras. After they moved a rock and shot pictures of the creatures under it, they returned the rock back to its place to protect the animals that lived there.

"It's my turn to get a picture," Susan said, poking her head out of the water. She swam around looking for one that might hide a special creature. *I want a large rock that's kind of flat,* she thought.

Susan saw the perfect rock. She lay in the water in front of it and signaled for Eric to lift it. As soon as he did, she started taking pictures. Suddenly, through the viewfinder, she saw a flash of red. Something was hurtling right at her. Splat! It hit her mask and hung on. She fell over onto her side, legs thrashing. Then she managed to scramble to her feet, but she kept on screaming and jumping about. "Get it off!" she cried.

Eric jumped up. Susan couldn't see him because of the red creature plastered across her mask, but she heard his camera clicking.

"Get it off!" she screamed again.

"Duck your head into the water," Eric yelled.

"I can't. I can't," Susan shouted, shaking her head back and forth. A red tentacle let go of her mask, dangled in front of her for a moment and then attached itself to her chin.

Susan screamed again.

"It's an octopus," Eric yelled, lunging at her. He dragged her down.

"Put your head into the water," he commanded, but this time he didn't wait for Susan to obey. He pushed her head into the water and then fell down beside her, still clicking his camera.

As soon as the octopus felt the water, it let go of Susan's mask, spit out a jet of purple ink, and disappeared. Susan and Eric stared into the little cloud of ink for a moment. Then Eric started turning every rock nearby as fast as he could, but the octopus had escaped.

They both stood up. "Wow!" they chorused together, and they laughed until their sides ached.

Eventually, Eric looked at the horizon. A red sun sat just above the water. "Let's head in," he said. "It's a long swim. Besides, I'm starving."

When they reached the shore and staggered out of the surf, Eric said, "I'm glad we looked closer."

"When we did, that place just exploded with life," Susan said, removing her mask. She looked up. Aunt Sally and Uncle Merle stood staring at them.

"We saw that you and the snorkel gear were missing," Uncle Merle explained. "When we walked out front, we heard you—or what we guessed must be you two—screaming and laughing."

"Then we saw you jumping around in the water," Aunt Sally said, throwing a towel to Susan and another one to Eric. "What did you find? You sure sounded excited."

"An octopus grabbed Susan by the mask," Eric said, getting a word in ahead of Susan. "You should have seen her dance."

"He pushed me into the water, and the octopus let go," Susan said.

"She still has a red spot where one tentacle stuck to her face," Eric said, pointing to Susan's chin.

Aunt Sally examined the red dot on Susan's face. "It's just a small spot," she said.

"Did you get any pictures?" Uncle Merle asked as they entered the cottage.

"I think so," Eric said. "I'll go download the memory card and see if one of them shows a small, red octopus." He doubled up again with laughter. Susan walked past him and yanked his wet hair. Then they ran up the stairs, leaving little pools of water behind them.

Fifteen minutes later, Eric ran into the hall. "You've got to see this," he yelled. Everyone gathered at his computer. A picture of a little red octopus plastered across Susan's mask filled the screen.

"Oh, no," Susan cried. "You aren't going to show that to anyone, are you?" But she couldn't help but smile at the sight of herself trying to rid her mask of the weird creature.

"Are you kidding? That could win a contest!" Eric said.

"Your eyes look like they might pop out of that mask any second," Uncle Merle said.

Eric clicked a button. "Look at that girl dance," he said, pointing to a picture of Susan leaping out of the water. Her ponytail stood straight out, both arms had shot high above her head, and her mouth was wide open. "You can even see the tentacle glued to her chin," Eric said. Then he fell on the floor, laughing and banging his fists into the carpet. Aunt Sally and Uncle Merle sat down on Eric's bed, threw their heads back, and laughed too.

Susan suddenly remembered that she had captured

some shots of Eric and the brittle stars. She ran to her room, grabbed her memory stick, and returned to Eric's room. She jammed it into the slot and sat in front of the computer. "This is Eric's adventure with the brittle stars," she said. Everyone leaned toward the screen. The picture they saw showed Eric leaping from the water, camera in hand. A small, hairy brittle star hung in the water, twitching. "The poor thing didn't know where to run for safety because Eric stirred up the water so much," Susan said.

When everyone stopped laughing enough for Uncle Merle to speak, he said, "Aunt Sally received a notice from Seven Seas Marine Institute today. They're offering a prize for the best series of twenty pictures with attached captions. The photographer has to select a theme, and the captions must be twenty-five to fifty words in length. The deadline to enter is next week. Mr. Wood was hoping you'd enter."

"You should do it, Eric," Susan said. "We saw all sorts of creatures hiding out. Maybe you could make that your theme."

"Um," Eric said. "I'll give that some thought."

"I haven't had a good laugh like that for weeks," Aunt Sally said. "But I think we should head downstairs for some supper."

"I learned something," Susan said after she had stuffed down a whole vegeburger. "I learned that God has provided a safe hiding place for every creature. They know where those places are, and they stick to them."

"Except when they get mixed up and land on a person's mask," Eric said, bursting into laughter again.

"Could you do a series on hiding places?" Susan said, ignoring Eric's antics. "We have the pictures of the shark in the cave, the brittle stars, and seashells."

"And a red octopus," Eric said, laughing again.

"It's true, Susan. God has provided some very interesting hiding places," Aunt Sally said.

"We have to look close to discover them," Uncle Merle said.

"She sure got close," Eric said, reaching over and yanking Susan's ponytail.

"I just realized something else," Susan said, making a face at Eric. "God also tucked His ideas into a safe place so I can discover them when I need them. He put them in the Bible."

"Good thinking," Uncle Merle said.

"Susan," Aunt Sally said, reaching into her pocket and pulling out a piece of yellow paper. "I know you're investigating God's ideas about spiritual gifts. I wrote these verses down for you. Check them out. Perhaps they will reveal a bit more of the mystery to you."

Susan's face lit up, and she stared at the paper.

"I'll do your share of the dishes," Eric said. "Go look up the verses."

"You'll do them if you can stop laughing long enough to stand in front of the sink," she said. Then she turned and headed up the stairs to her room.

The list of verses Aunt Sally gave Susan started with Ephesians 4. Susan grabbed a Bible, sat down, and found that chapter. Verses 7 and 8 told her that in this place the Bible was talking about gifts that Jesus gave His people when He ascended to heaven. Verse 10 said He "went into the highest heaven, so that he would fill the whole universe."

Wow! Susan thought. *Jesus fills the whole universe! I like that, because it means that wherever I go, He's with me.*

She read the next verse: "Christ chose some of us to be apostles, prophets, missionaries, pastors, and teachers." For a moment, she felt disappointed. Ephesians 4 didn't list Eric's gift, and it didn't mention a gift that fit her either. Then she remembered that Aunt Sally had written down two other Bible passages. Both Romans 12 and 1 Corinthians 12 listed several spiritual gifts. When Susan compared the lists, she realized that none of them were exactly the same.

I know, she thought, *the Bible is just giving examples of the different kinds of gifts. So, there could be many gifts besides the ones it names!* In fact, 1 Corinthians 12:7 told her, "The Spirit has given each of us a special way of serving others." She jumped up, whirled around, and sat down again. Then her eyes flew back to the Bible.

She turned back to Ephesians 4. Verses 12 and 13 said that Jesus gave the spiritual gifts "so that his people would learn to serve and his body would grow strong. This will continue until we are united by our faith and by our understanding of the Son of God. Then we will be mature, just as Christ is, and we will be completely like him."

Susan knew that Jesus' "body" means His church. These verses helped her understand the reason Jesus gives spiritual gifts to the people who love Him. He wants His people, His church, to grow to be like Him. He also wants them to be strong enough to do the job He has given them. She knew that is to tell people the good news about Jesus.

Then she read verse 14: "We must not let deceitful people trick us by their false teachings, which are like winds that toss us around from place to place."

Spiritual gifts are just like an anchor, Susan thought, remembering how good she felt when she saw the anchor line at Babylon Reef. *Using my gifts will be like being anchored in a wild, tossing sea. It will keep me from being confused, and it will give me purpose and joy.*

Then she sighed and said to herself, "But what are my gifts?"

"Did you figure it out?" Eric asked as he entered Susan's room and plunked himself onto the floor near her.

"Not yet," Susan said. "But I know some things. I know that everyone has a gift and that God gives gifts so His body, the church, will be strong and able to do the work of sharing the good news about Jesus with others. I also know that when I use my gifts, I will grow and have more joy."

"That's a lot to know," Eric said. "I think God's plan is a good one even though we don't understand all of it yet."

"Hey, I thought of a good title for your theme," Susan said. "How about 'God's Hidden Treasures'?"

"I like that," Eric said, getting up. "I think I'll gather some pictures that might fit into that theme. Keep searching, Susan. You'll find your treasure soon. Just don't get too close!" Then he dashed out the door before Susan could grab him. "Don't get too close," he said again, slamming his door.

It certainly will be a surprise when I do discover it, Susan thought, remembering the tiny, round suction cups pressed against her mask. *Maybe I'm close to it right now.*

Susan placed her Bible on the nightstand and pulled *Island Adventure* from beneath her pillow. *I have enough time to read one chapter before bedtime,* she thought. When she opened the book, a small, white envelope fell out. Susan picked it up. She saw the word *Sally* written on it. *This note belongs to Aunt Sally,* she thought. *I shouldn't read it.* But she found her fingers already reaching into the envelope.

"Dear Sally, Thanks for being a wonderful friend and helping me get this set of books printed. Thanks for the idea of using a pen name. The—"

Susan stopped reading. She felt sure Aunt Sally wouldn't want her to read the note without her permission. But she couldn't help noticing the name "Carol" signed at the bottom of the note.

Susan jammed the note into the envelope and tucked it into the book. Then she slammed the cover shut. She knew she shouldn't have read any of the note. She felt guilty, but she couldn't resist trying to understand the mystery. *So "Judith Smith" is a pen name,* she thought. *Then who is the real author? Why would the author use a pen name? If I wrote great books like this, I'd want my real name plastered on the front cover.*

The answers were hidden, like little treasures, and Susan wanted to uncover them all. She decided she would let Aunt Sally see her reading the book and allow the note to fall out. Then she would hand the note to Aunt Sally. If Aunt Sally wanted to share the information in it with her, she would.

So many hidden treasures, Susan thought, yawning. *I've gotten close to some of them and too close to one in particular. Tomorrow I'll uncover some more.* And with that, her eyelids closed. Then, after what seemed to be about a minute, she heard Eric shouting, "Get up, Susan. We're heading for Turtle Reef."

CHAPTER 6

TERROR AT TURTLE REEF

Aunt Sally and Susan packed lunches while Uncle Merle and Eric stowed gear in the car. Then they drove down the Queen's Highway along the coast.

"Eric and Susan, you carry the empty tanks to the back door," Uncle Merle said as they approached the Eden Rock dive shop. "Check with Dorothy, and then load up ten full tanks. Use this gauge to check each tank. The needle should move up to at least the three-thousand mark. Aunt Sally and I will go inside and purchase some new O-rings for the cameras. Got to keep that ocean water out."

"OK," the twins chorused. When Uncle Merle had parked the car, Eric jumped out and opened the back of the station wagon. He and Susan toted the empty tanks to the shop door and placed them in a long line against the wall near the door.

"Hello," Dorothy called. She stood near the rinse tank, helping a couple of divers select BCDs. "The full tanks are standing near the compressor," she said. "Take ten of them."

"Thanks," Eric said. Then he headed for the compressor, where two men were filling tanks with compressed air. "They're sure heavy," he sighed. "I'm glad Uncle Merle parked close. Susan, please stand the tanks by the bumper. I'll load them."

Susan watched as Eric laid five tanks flat, placed a beach towel over them and arranged five more on top.

"I have to use this gauge to double-check the level of air in these tanks," he said.

"OK," Susan said, heading for the edge of the concrete platform, where several divers were preparing to go out.

Eric tested six tanks. Each held three thousand pounds of air. The hot sun beat down on his head. "How's the water?" he called to Susan.

"Clear and calm," Susan yelled back. "I wish we could dive right here and right now. It's so hot."

"I have to check four more tanks," Eric said, wiping his forehead.

"Hurry up," Susan said. "Let's slip down the ladder and take a quick swim. Aunt Sally always takes a long time in the dive shop."

Eric could almost feel the cool sea washing over him. "OK, but just a quick one," he said, glancing toward Susan. He turned and looked down at the tanks for a moment and then slammed the tailgate of the station wagon shut. He joined Susan at the ladder, and they climbed down.

Susan sank into the water. It felt wonderful. She didn't care that Eric splashed tons of water at her. Moments later, they heard Uncle Merle and Aunt Sally calling them. They hurried up the ladder and ran to the car. "I bet that felt good," Uncle Merle said, laughing. "Let's go. I'm ready to leap into the sea."

"Turtle Reef got its name because it sits offshore from the Cayman Turtle Farm," Aunt Sally said. "Would you like to stop there for a few minutes before we dive?"

"Yes!" the twins chorused.

Uncle Merle stopped the car. He disappeared into a building and returned carrying four tickets. He gave one to each of them, and they headed for the big, round, wooden tanks that lay scattered around the property.

"These turtles aren't any bigger than a moon jelly," Susan said, splashing her hands in one of the tanks. She reached out and picked up a little turtle. It looked at her and twitched its legs about.

Eric dashed to another tank and peered in. "These are huge," he called. "They're almost as big as a stingray."

When Susan joined Eric and looked into the tank, she couldn't believe her eyes. At least thirty turtles swirled about in the tank. She kept her hands out of their reach.

"What do they do with them?" Susan asked when they tired of looking at the turtles and headed for the dive site.

"They release the turtles into the sea," Aunt Sally said. "I think they might use some of them for food."

"That's terrible!" Susan said.

"At least no one is out there catching the wild turtles, so we have a good chance of seeing one," Uncle Merle said. "Suit up! That water is calling me."

Susan laid out her gear. She took longer then the others to prepare, but she wanted to be sure she connected everything right. She looked over at Eric. He almost threw things together. She had never seen him work so fast. He donned his BCD and tank and grabbed his fins and mask. "I'm off," he said to Susan. "See you at the ladder."

"Hold it. I haven't checked your tank," Susan said, reaching out to open the air valve on Eric's tank.

"Already got it," Eric said, dodging her hand.

Susan watched him walk away. He didn't wait for her as he usually did. *He won't dare go off by himself,* she thought.

Aunt Sally and Uncle Merle started down the ladder, and Susan followed.

She climbed down into a small cove almost closed in by coral formations.

The four of them stood in a circle facing each other in the shallow water. "This area is ringed in by a series of walls covered by coral," Uncle Merle said. "We'll float out on our backs and descend to about thirty feet. This small reef formation contains lots of sea life, so look close. When we make the horseshoe loop, we'll ascend and swim together back through this narrow entrance to the cove and climb up the ladder."

Uncle Merle reached out and turned Aunt Sally's air on. Eric opened Susan's valve. She shot a glance at her air gauge. It read three thousand. They all puffed air into their BCDs and floated out to sea. "I'm going to get a shot of a turtle," Eric said as he paddled past Susan.

A hundred feet from shore, they descended to the reef. *It isn't flat like Babylon Reef,* Susan thought. Instead of lying on their stomachs and swimming over the reef, they stood in the water in front of the reef wall and stared at the corals.

Every few minutes, Eric turned away from the reef and looked all around. *He's checking for turtles,* Susan thought. She watched him turn back toward the wall of coral and sea fans. He focused on a tiny fairy basslet that darted back and forth, shouting purple and yellow. Eric pointed to the fish and then at Susan. She made a face at him through her mask.

Susan glanced over at Aunt Sally and Uncle Merle. They moved slowly along the wall. A few seconds later, she looked over to see Eric, but he had disappeared. She swirled around in a full circle. She didn't see Eric anywhere, and she counted only three streams of bubbles rising toward the surface. Even if he had chased a turtle to the far side of the coral formation, she should be able to see his bubbles. Then she looked up toward the surface. Eric was rising up slowly, his eyes as big as jellyfish.

Susan waved her arms around trying to get Uncle Merle's attention. She started to ascend while signaling over and over, hoping he would see her. She resisted the urge to kick her fins and jet upward. She noticed that when Eric reached the surface, he didn't burst through. He hung just below it, kicking furiously. She saw him fumble with his pocket and watched a lead weight fall through the water beside her. Still, Eric didn't break the surface. He looked down at her with wide eyes and thrashed his hand across his throat. *He's giving me the "out of air" signal,* she thought. *He needs help.*

Susan kicked her fins and ascended as fast as she dared. She grabbed the dive knife that she had strapped to her leg on every dive but never used. She reached around with it and banged it on her tank. Then she looked down. Aunt Sally and Uncle Merle had heard the strange noise. They spotted her and began to rise toward the surface.

In seconds, Susan arrived at Eric's side. She reached into her pocket and grabbed her spare air regulator, jamming it into Eric's mouth. She remembered to hang on to the hose with one hand in case Eric panicked and tried to tear it away from her.

Eric gulped air. He settled down, hanging just below the surface and facing Susan. His eyes said, "Thank you."

Uncle Merle broke through the surface. He reached out and found the air hose that connected to Eric's BCD. He puffed air into it. The vest inflated and lifted Eric out of the water so he could breathe. Eric spit out Susan's spare regulator and gasped. Susan added air to her BCD and burst through the surface beside him. Then Aunt Sally joined them. "What's going on?" she asked, staring at Eric.

"I ran out of air," Eric gasped.

"Of all the things that could go wrong, this is totally preventable, Sally," Uncle Merle said, staring at Eric.

"No one is hurt," Aunt Sally soothed. "Let's talk about this later. Head in. This dive is aborted."

"Sorry," Susan mouthed to Eric as they swam toward shore.

Eric smiled weakly and laid his head back, kicking small strokes. Susan stayed close beside him. Gradually, Eric's breathing slowed down.

One by one, they climbed the ladder, removed their gear, and carried it to the car. Eric slumped down onto the backseat, and Susan joined him. When they drove away, Susan looked back at the shimmering blue sea. *Eric won't see a turtle today,* she thought, and she sighed.

Susan hated the next ten minutes. They usually talked and laughed about the discoveries they had made on their dive, but now no one spoke. She watched the small waves crash onto the shore as they rode along. "This dive is aborted," they seemed to say mockingly. *Wow,* Susan thought. *Diving can be scary.* She looked over at Eric. He turned away and stared out the opposite window. *He could have died,* she thought.

"We need to discuss the accident," Aunt Sally said when they reached their house. Her voice was calm but firm. "Talking about it will help us understand what went wrong and what we need to do to prevent it from happening again."

"Susan, why didn't you check Eric's air supply before we entered the water?" Uncle Merle asked. He turned for a second, and his gaze pierced right through her. He wore the biggest frown she had ever seen.

"It's my fault," Eric said. "Susan tried to check me, but I was in a hurry to get into the water. I wanted to be the first one to see a turtle."

"Susan," Uncle Merle's voice had softened. "It's your responsibility to check your partner's gear and air supply no matter what. However, some partners don't make it very easy, do they, son?" he said, glancing at Eric.

"No, sir." Eric mumbled.

"Your tank didn't last very long," Aunt Sally said. "I had more than two thousand pounds of air left when I ascended."

"I . . . I didn't check all the tanks at the dive shop like you asked me to," Eric admitted. "The tank I used must not have been full."

"Eric," Uncle Merle said, shaking his head, "you endangered each of us."

"I was wrong and careless, sir," Eric said. He didn't give Uncle Merle a bunch of excuses. "I'm sorry, everyone," he said.

"An accident like this should never happen," Uncle Merle commented. "But that being said, I'm very happy about how you and Susan handled it."

"You are?" they blurted, looking at each other.

"First, Susan, you didn't go ballistic and blast off to the surface, blowing out your eardrums. You thought to bang on your tank, and you signaled Aunt Sally and me as you ascended. When you got to the surface, you remembered to share your air source and hang on to the hose in case Eric panicked. Good going!"

Susan smiled, and she looked over at Eric.

"Thanks, Susan," he said, patting her hand. "You saved me. I was in the death zone."

"The death zone?" Susan asked, her eyes getting big.

"When I realized that my air was almost gone, I signaled you and started going up. I kept blowing out slowly as we learned to do at the dive school. I pressed the button that lets air from the tank into the vest, but nothing happened. Then I tried to kick hard enough to lift my head out of the water so that I could blow air into my BCD, but I hung too low in the water. I call it the death zone because I couldn't breathe beneath the water, and I couldn't get myself high enough to breathe out of it."

"Oh, Eric," Susan said, a tear running down her cheek.

"Goodness," Aunt Sally gasped.

"Eric did the right thing," Aunt Sally said after another long silence. "He dropped some weight to allow himself to rise up."

"He didn't panic either," Uncle Merle said. "As a result of the actions you both took, you avoided a disaster."

"I hope we have all learned something today," Aunt Sally said.

"I've learned something," Eric said, looking at the others. "Check and recheck—that's my motto from now on."

"What we all need right now is a shower and a hot meal," Uncle Merle said. "Eric and I will unload the gear if you girls will get started on supper."

"Sounds like a plan," Aunt Sally said, smiling. Uncle Merle reached out and hugged her close. *She was frightened today,* Susan thought as she followed Aunt Sally into the kitchen. *I was scared too, but I didn't panic.*

"Eric," Uncle Merle said, "please check the tanks. We'll use four of them tomorrow night. I'll store the empty ones in the laundry room."

"Yes, sir," Eric said.

Eric placed the gauge onto each tank. He didn't quit until he had seen for himself that each tank held three thousand pounds. "All done, Uncle Merle," he said, toting Susan's bag into the laundry. He filled the big tub and dumped all the dive gear into it.

After supper, Susan and Eric hung their dive gear out to dry and then went to their rooms. Susan curled up on her bed. She had just reached for the book *Island Adventure* when she heard Aunt Sally knock on her door.

"Susan," Aunt Sally said, "may I come in for a moment?"

"Of course," Susan said, sitting up. She didn't hide the book.

"I just want to tell you how proud I am," Aunt Sally said, sitting on the bed. "You really kept your wits about you. I'd be glad to be your dive partner anytime."

"Thank you, Aunt Sally," Susan said. "I probably would have panicked, but I prayed for help. All the stuff that I did just popped into my mind."

"You did the right thing," Aunt Sally said.

"I learned something out there," Susan said. "Air is life. A diver needs to know he has lots of air at all times. I think prayer is like that. It helps us stay connected to Jesus, who is our Lifeline."

"You're certainly right, Susan," Aunt Sally said, reaching out and giving her a big hug before heading for the door.

"Good night, Aunt Sally," Susan said.

Susan listened to Aunt Sally's footsteps fade away. She started to pick up her book, but Eric walked in. "Susan," he said, "I need help. Would you look over this set of pictures for me? If you have any suggestions, let me know. I might enter them in the contest."

"Sure," Susan said. "Just lay the disk beside my computer. I'll get to them first thing in the morning."

"Thanks, Susan," Eric said. He hesitated at the door a moment, looking at her, and then he walked out.

Susan got up and shoved the disk into her computer. She stared at the pictures. Eric did have a way of getting the right composition, lighting, and clarity in each picture. And his pictures always made her laugh. But when she read the captions beneath the pictures, she shook her head. Eric just didn't have a way with words. She started erasing the captions and replacing them with words that complemented the pictures. Before long, she was lost in her work. She spotted the picture of the red octopus and laughed. She relived the event in her mind. That helped her select the best words to describe the experience.

After several hours, she stopped and stretched. *This is really fun,* she admitted to herself. *But I'd better stop now and finish doing this tomorrow. If I stay up late, I'll be too tired to dive.*

The next morning Susan awoke early. As the tropical sun eased over the horizon and into the sky and a warm breeze flowed through her window, she sat in front of the computer and opened the picture file. Before long, she forgot about everything except selecting the best words for each picture. *I really like this,* she thought.

"Where's Susan?" Aunt Sally said, her voice reaching up the stairs and into Susan's room.

"She's helping me with some stuff," Susan heard Eric say.

Susan laughed to herself. She was usually the first one to sit down at the breakfast table. Yet today, she hadn't even thought about eating. All she cared about was working with words. "The desire and ability to use words can be a gift," an inner voice suggested. "You love to work with words."

Susan stopped typing and sat still. She stared at the screen, but she didn't see the pictures. *Could the ability to work with words be a gift?* she wondered. She realized for the first time just how much she did love words. She remembered that she often selected what words she might use to describe the things she saw in the reef even before she got out of the water. *I'm as excited about words as Eric is about his pictures,* she thought.

Susan looked at the captions again. The choice of words made a big difference—it surprised her just how much of a difference. An excitement crept over her. Judith Smith knew how to use words to draw her readers into a story. Words had power.

Susan stared at the screen for a long time without seeing it. Finally, she stood up, walked to the window, and opened it. The sound of the surf filtered into the room. *Words are strong, like the surf,* she thought. And suddenly she knew what she wanted to do. "I'm going to use words to help people know God better," she said out loud. She danced around the room and then fell on her knees beside her bed. "Thank You for helping me figure it out, God," she said. "I see that You have been showing me little by little for a long time. I know You'll show me more later."

All at once Susan wanted to tell everyone, yet at the same time she didn't want to. She felt like shouting, but she also felt like curling up on her bed and pulling the covers over her head so she could press the new ideas to herself in secret.

"Susan," Eric called from the kitchen, "are you almost done?"

"Coming right down," Susan said, trying to keep the excitement out of her voice.

She retrieved the disk and ran down the stairs. When she entered the kitchen, she handed the disk to Eric. "These are good," she said. "I know you can win that contest."

"I didn't say I would enter for sure," Eric said. Then he stared at her and said, "What's up with you?"

"Nothing," Susan said, glancing away.

"Hey, I'm your twin. I know when something is up. I say something is going on that you aren't talking about."

"There's nothing going on," Susan insisted.

"You figured it out, didn't you? I can see it written all over your face," he said, smiling.

"I don't want to talk about it yet," Susan blurted.

"Yes you do," Eric teased.

"OK, you're right," Susan admitted. "I think using words is my gift. I love them the way you love your photographs. I can paint pictures with them. Words are powerful."

"Wow!" Eric said. "I bet you're going to be a writer like Aunt Sally. I can't wait to tell her."

"Don't say anything," Susan pleaded. "I'll tell her later."

"OK," Eric agreed. "But I bet Aunt Sally will figure it out all by herself."

"Susan. Eric," Uncle Merle called, coming into the kitchen. "Don't forget to take two flashlights tonight."

"And don't forget to double-check your batteries," Aunt Sally added, joining the others. "Say, what's going on?"

"Told you," Eric said, heading for his room.

"I'll get my gear and check my lights," Susan said, following Eric up the stairs. "We'll be right back down for breakfast."

As they climbed the stairs, Susan heard Aunt Sally say to Uncle Merle, "I don't know what they're up to, but they looked awfully happy about something."

CHAPTER 7

MYSTERIOUS LIGHT

After their dive the next day, ideas and memories spun around in Susan's head. She didn't want any of them to escape. So as soon as she shed her dive suit, she wrapped herself in a towel, grabbed her notebook, and plopped down onto the backseat of the car. And when her pen hit the paper, words spilled from her mind like waves upon the beach.

Aunt Sally and Uncle Merle glanced at her several times but said nothing. Eric smiled to himself. He picked up her gear bag and tossed it into the car.

Fifteen minutes into their drive back to their cottage, Susan closed her notebook and put away her pen. "Aunt Sally," she said, "please stop at the market. I need to get another notebook."

"Have you used that one up already?" Aunt Sally said, looking at Susan.

"I'll be glad to stop," Uncle Merle said, casting Aunt Sally a glance.

When Uncle Merle stopped the car, Susan leaped out and headed for the store. "She's forgotten that she is sopping wet and her hair is a mess," Aunt Sally said. "That isn't like her."

No one spoke. Soon they saw Susan exit the store carrying a large bag.

"Got everything?" Uncle Merle asked, staring at the bag.

"I bought several notebooks so you won't have to stop again," Susan said.

An hour later, Eric found Susan sitting on her bed and scribbling as fast as she could. He smiled to himself. "Better get ready," he said. "We're going to dive Eden Rock tonight. Uncle Merle says you need two dive lights."

Susan felt excited about the notes she had taken. She hated to tear herself away from her writing, but she knew she needed to check her equipment list. She hurried about, gathering up her gear so she could get back to her writing. She found two dive lights, attached one to the Velcro patch on the front of her BCD and placed the larger one in her dive bag. She was ready.

Soon she sat in front of the computer again. She looked at every sentence, reworking them to sound better. She read a chapter in the creative writing book she had chosen from Aunt Sally's bookcase and then reworked her sentences again, choosing stronger verbs and specific nouns that painted vivid pictures.

Several times Aunt Sally peeked into her room. Susan didn't notice.

"We're leaving," Eric called, interrupting her concentration. Susan looked out the window. The sun had dropped toward the horizon. "I'm coming," she shouted back, pushing the notebook under her pillow. She grabbed her dive bag and headed down the stairs.

By the time they reached Eden Rock, the sun rested on the water, and red and yellow streaked the sky. The sea sat silent and calm, reflecting back the colors splashed upon it by the sun, and a playful breeze danced among the palm trees. "Perfect evening for a dive," Uncle Merle said, gathering his gear together and heading for the dive platform.

It is beautiful, Susan thought as she struggled into her suit. She watched Eric check each piece of equipment. He opened the valve on his air tank and looked at the pressure gauge. Susan smiled. *He's being careful,* she thought.

They entered the sea as the sun slipped beneath the horizon. The water looked darker than during the day. *It's trying to hold on to some of the fading sunlight,* Susan thought. *I wonder what it will look like down here when the light is gone.* The thought of darkness closing in nudged her to check again that her dive light hung at her side. She moved closer to Aunt Sally.

As they descended, four dive lights popped on. The darkness snuffed out all but a small circle of light around each of them. Susan wanted to ascend into the daylight, but then she remembered that by now it was dark on the surface. She glanced around. She could see streams of light from Uncle Merle's and Eric's dive lights and the glow of their camera strobes. They hung in front of a coral formation. She moved closer.

A clump of long, tangled tubes sat on the end of a lettuce coral that stuck out from the reef. Susan watched the tubes unfurl. Each one held shorter tubes that also uncurled. "Basket star," Uncle Merle wrote on his slate. He held the slate up to Susan. She nodded. The sea star unwound itself until it looked like a beautiful flower clinging to the coral. Eric clicked away. Susan could see his smile in the dim light.

They moved along, following the yellow trail created by the dive lights. Suddenly, they spotted an octopus a short distance away. It spread itself against the coral, and its tentacles coiled and uncoiled. Each tentacle worked independently of the others, reaching into crevices and beneath small rocks. The octopus oozed along the reef, flashing green and brown colors. Then, suddenly, it flung itself out into the darkness. Eric's light followed it.

Susan hung in the water, staring at the creature whose tentacles shot out in different directions, changing its shape every second. The octopus watched her, its eyes glowing red in the beam of light from Eric's camera. It swirled around, unfolding its tentacles, and the thin web of flesh between them stretched out, forming a great umbrella. Then it drew each tentacle to its body, making itself into a large, brown, speckled ball. It squeezed into a small space in the reef, and one tentacle reached out and clutched a clump of star coral.

Susan almost forgot to breath. She stayed right behind Eric and turned the ray of her light away so it wouldn't interfere with his camera light. All at once, the octopus slithered out of the crevice. It pulled its tentacles forward, ahead of its body, and then shot them back together, blasting itself away like a rocket into the darkness.

When the twitching mass of green and brown disappeared, the dive team stayed still for a moment. Then they turned and moved back toward the reef. Susan directed her light ahead of her, its ray boring a white hole into the dark water. Then suddenly it blinked off. Susan shook the light. Nothing happened. She glanced around her. She couldn't see Uncle Merle, Aunt Sally, or Eric. But she could see three spots of light moving slowly away from her.

Susan drew in a deep breath and tried to hurry to catch the fading lights. Even though she knew that in a moment someone would glance around to check on her, she felt a great fear envelope her as darkness closed in. She felt as if she were hanging inside a great ball of wet blackness where she couldn't tell up from down. The lights ahead of her became fainter and fainter. *What if I bang into a coral pillar? What if a shark crashes into me? No one will know,* she thought. She kicked her fins harder and moved faster. Then the lights stopped moving forward and shot about in the darkness. *They're looking for me,* she thought, and she waved her arms.

The lights moved toward her. Uncle Merle reached through the darkness and took her dive light. He fiddled with it for a moment and then dropped it into his small equipment bag. Eric flashed his light into her face, blinding her for a moment, but she didn't care—the light felt wonderful. Eric grabbed the small dive light attached to her BCD, turned it on, and handed it to her. A small beam of light shot out. It looked like a thin, yellow line in the great blackness about her.

Uncle Merle motioned for her to stay beside him, and they swam on together—three large beams and one skinny streak of light moving through the night. Susan tried to get her mind off the darkness and focus on the tiny cleaner shrimp that Eric caught in his camera light. *What happens if this small light goes out?* she thought, clutching it so tightly that her fingers hurt.

Uncle Merle and Aunt Sally kept Susan between them. They moved deeper and deeper into the sea. *I hate the darkness. I hate the reef at night,* Susan thought, but she kept moving.

Uncle Merle stopped. "Small cave," he wrote on his dive slate. Then he made the dive sign that meant "follow me."

Susan wanted to surface. She wanted to see the tropical sun burning like a torch. She didn't want to go into a cave. But she didn't want to stay outside the cave by herself with her tiny light either. She felt sure that if it went out, no one would ever find her out there in the dark sea.

Susan followed Uncle Merle and the others through a tunnel that seemed to go on forever. She imagined how it would feel to become lost in the cave, run out of air, and die deep under the water. She tried to memorize some of the marks along the way that she might have to follow to get out again. *I have to stop thinking like this or I won't enjoy any part of this dive,* she thought. But in the dim light, her thoughts darkened.

After a few minutes, they entered a large room. Susan saw Eric cast his light about the cave walls, searching for sea creatures. At first, Susan felt disappointed that she didn't see a single fish. Then she worried that she would. What if a barracuda, caught by surprise in the small space, attacked them? She swallowed an urge to scream.

Uncle Merle touched her shoulder and motioned for her to sit down. Susan tried to obey, but her body wanted to float. She struggled to gather her arms and legs together. Then she remembered to let all the air out of her lungs for a second, and she felt herself settle to the floor of the cave. Then she breathed in and out in regular breaths and managed to stay put.

Just as Susan began to feel comfortable, Aunt Sally motioned for them to switch off their lights. Susan couldn't believe it. Why would anyone want to shut off a light while inside a dark cave fifty feet down in the night sea? She shook her head No and clutched her light tightly. Aunt Sally drew Susan close beside her and directed the beam from Susan's dive light onto her dive slate. "It will be OK," she wrote. Then Uncle Merle waved one of his arms through the darkness that surrounded him. Susan gasped. Thousands of miniature lights blinked on. Susan could see Uncle Merle's face behind the light. He wore a big grin.

Eric clapped his hands together, and lights shot on. Susan stared. She switched off her light but kept her finger on the button. Then she swirled her free arm in a big circle. Tiny pinpricks of light blazed in the darkness. As soon as she stopped moving, the lights faded. Susan laughed. She pressed her dive light onto the patch of Velcro on her dive suit so she could use both of her hands to swish the water. Then everyone tried to outdo the others and make the most light. Susan painted circles of light in the black water, and she made loops and squares.

Long before Susan wanted to leave, Uncle Merle signaled for them to follow him. They all switched on their lights and moved single file toward the entrance of the cave. As they swam along, Susan felt joy well up inside her. Every miniature light made a difference, and when the lights blazed together, they made a great light that erased her fears.

When they were back in open water, Uncle Merle signaled for them to surface. Susan floated upward, keeping her eyes on her gauges so she wouldn't rise too fast. When she burst into the night air, a full moon glowed down upon her and thousands of stars sparkled in the sky. *God is incredible,* she thought. Suddenly, light seemed like the most wonderful thing in the whole world.

They floated on their backs and kicked their way toward shore. "I learned something," Susan said.

"I bet you learned to double-check your batteries before diving, and that you need to get a bigger secondary light than that little thing," Eric said, jabbing at the small, pink light attached to Susan's vest.

"That's true," Susan admitted. "But I also discovered a formula."

"Let's hear it," Eric said, kicking his fins and moving next to her.

"A big light equals small fear, and a small light equals big fear," she said. "I plan on buying the biggest light I can find before I go down there again at night."

"Good one, Susan," Uncle Merle said. He threw his head back and laughed, and his laughter brightened the night. Susan couldn't help but laugh too.

"Seriously," Susan said as they floated along, "darkness is a terrible thing. But if you have enough light, it doesn't matter. You live in the light, not in the darkness."

"Were you scared when your light went out?" Eric asked.

"I was terrified," Susan admitted. "I imagined that I was lost in a sea full of awful creatures."

"I learned something too," Eric said. "God isn't just the Light of the world; He's the Light of the sea. Uncle Merle, what made that light?"

"Scientists call it bioluminescence. Light doesn't filter down deeper than two or three thousand feet. Many creatures live in the deep abyss, so God gave them the ability to make light."

"The fish that create light do so with special cells called photophores," Aunt Sally explained. "Some light is made by bacteria that live in symbiotic relationship with the fish."

"These fish can turn the light on and off and even change white light into different colors," Uncle Merle said.

"What do they use the light for?" Susan asked, tugging off her fins as they neared the dive ladder.

"They use them to attract a mate, confuse an enemy, or find food," Uncle Merle explained.

"Or entertain a bunch of scared people in a dark cave," Eric said, following Susan up the ladder.

"So you were scared too," Susan said.

"I was not," Eric objected. "But I like the sea better in the daylight. Things look better in the light."

"Speaking of light," Aunt Sally said as they loaded the car. "When we begin to understand something that has bothered us for a while, it's like someone has switched on a light in a dark room. You've been looking rather bright lately, Susan."

Susan stared at Aunt Sally, her face lighting up without her permission. *Aunt Sally knows I've discovered something important,* she thought. *She's trying to wait for me to bring the subject up.* She cast a glance at Eric. He smiled. "Told you," he said.

Susan hadn't thought about her discovery for several hours; she had just enjoyed a strong sense of peace. Now the joy inside her pushed words out of her mouth, and she couldn't stop them. "I'm going to be a writer," she blurted. "I love words. They're powerful. They paint pictures. They teach. I want to use them to help others learn about God. There are a lot of people wandering around in darkness. They don't understand how much God loves them. If I write about what I learn in the ocean, maybe they will see God in a new light and not be so afraid of Him. That's what makes me excited."

"Well!" Aunt Sally exclaimed.

"She figured it out," Eric said, smiling.

Uncle Merle pulled the car off the road and parked in front of a supermarket. Red and yellow lights blinked on and off in the night, casting a glow on the hood of the car. No one spoke for a moment. "This is a special moment," he said, turning in his seat and looking at Susan. "Not everyone strives so hard to understand this important truth. You wanted to know and understand. God has certainly shined His light into your mind. He will continue to teach you the direction He wants you to go. I'm so glad, Susan."

Then Uncle Merle started up the car, and they drove off. The headlights pierced the darkness, and they followed the beams home.

Aunt Sally didn't say a word, but Susan could see tears forming in her eyes. "I wonder what she's thinking," Susan whispered to Eric.

When they reached the house, they all hugged each other, said Good night, and headed to bed. Susan realized that she felt different. She no longer felt confused. A weight had lifted from her heart, and new possibilities danced in her head.

Susan thought she'd read for a few minutes before going to sleep. Just as she picked up the book *Island Adventures*, Aunt Sally appeared in her doorway. "Come in," Susan said, and she raised a hand to motion Aunt Sally in. As she did so, a small envelope fell from the book and tumbled onto the floor.

Aunt Sally stooped and picked up the envelope. But instead of looking at it, she looked at Susan. She reached down and grabbed Susan, hugging her. "I'm really happy about your discovery," she said. "It's a wonderful thing to have a dream. I'll do anything I can to help you reach your goals." Then she sat down and looked at the envelope in her hand. "Oh," she said, "this is mine."

When Aunt Sally opened the envelope and read the note, tears filled eyes. She glanced at Susan and then reached out, took the book from Susan's hand, and stared at the title. "I suppose you've read this note," she said.

"I started to," Susan admitted. "But I decided that it wasn't my note, so I put it back in the book."

"Good," Aunt Sally said returning the book to Susan. "I guess I better get going. It's time to sleep."

"Why did the author use a pen name?" Susan blurted at Aunt Sally's back.

Aunt Sally stopped. She didn't turn toward Susan. "Authors sometimes choose to do that for various reasons," she said, and then she just walked away.

Susan got up. She stood in her doorway and watched Aunt Sally disappear into her room. She heard Uncle Merle say, "You've got to talk to her some time."

Susan turned back into her room and climbed onto her bed. *Why did Aunt Sally just walk off?* she wondered. *Why did Uncle Merle say Aunt Sally should talk to me?*

Susan sighed. She really had learned important things while on that dive. For one thing, she knew she didn't like darkness—not in the water nor in her mind. God would be her light. When dark thoughts threatened to engulf her, He would shine His light into her mind. She took a deep breath and fell asleep.

CHAPTER 8

THE SECRET

Susan awoke when a sunbeam danced across her face. She had placed the book *Island Adventure* on the nightstand the night before. Now, she picked it up and stared at it. She imagined that she saw her own name printed on the front. "Someday," she whispered.

"Are you going to stay in bed all day?" Eric called through her doorway.

"Of course not," Susan snapped. "But I sure would like a minute to myself."

However, Eric didn't go away. He had something on his mind. "Last night I heard Uncle Merle tell Aunt Sally that she should talk to you about something," he said. "They're keeping something from us. You must feel like you're sitting on a fire coral."

"I don't feel like that at all," Susan retorted.

"Aren't you dying to know what the big secret is?" Eric asked. He plopped himself onto the rug beside Susan's bed. "Aunt Sally isn't her usual cheerful self."

"There isn't any secret," Susan said. "You're imagining things."

"No, I'm not," Eric said. "Aunt Sally's lips are pressed

together tighter than a clam. She has been staring out one window or another all morning."

"I just asked her why the author of this book used a pen name," Susan said.

"You mean Judith Smith isn't the author?" Eric said, grabbing the book from Susan and staring at the front cover.

"I don't know who the author is. 'Judith Smith' is a pen name," Susan replied. "When Aunt Sally realized that I had read part of the note that was tucked inside the book, she just walked out."

"Maybe she didn't want to discuss the note," Eric suggested.

"I wish I had read it," Susan said.

"Aunt Sally will probably talk about it later," Eric said. "Let's go and look at the pictures of the creatures we saw on our night dive."

"Good idea," Susan said, feeling relieved to get off the subject. She tucked the book under her arm and followed Eric to his room. When she sat down beside Eric in front of the computer, she placed the book on the desk.

Eric opened his picture file. "Look at these lobsters," he said, laughing. "I saw them marching around on the sand. At night they leave their hiding places under ledges and crawl all over the place."

"They twitch too much for me," Susan said. "But I love the red crabs. They look almost like people when they use their tiny pinchers to eat."

"Look at this shot," Eric said, pointing to a picture of two mollusk creatures called flamingo tongues that were peeking from their shells. "Aunt Sally says they actually eat part of the sea fans. She said the fans can grow back, so it doesn't actually harm them."

"What's that red, feathery thing?" Susan asked, staring at a picture of a clam with long red tentacles swishing around.

"That's Lima scabra," Eric explained. "It's a bivalve mollusk that attaches itself to a hard surface. It's filter feeding. I saw its picture in a book," he said, looking at Susan.

"How does it attach to the rock?" Susan asked.

"It spins byssus threads," Eric said. "They're thin and strong. I think it makes a lot of them instead of one or two thick ones."

Susan smiled. "Jesus is my Rock, and I want to attach to Him," she said.

"I get it," Eric said. "Every time I talk to God or read from His Word, it's like spinning a silver thread between Jesus and me. The more, the better."

"You're beginning to sound like Aunt Sally," Susan said, and she laughed.

Suddenly, a message popped up on the computer screen. "You have mail!" it said.

"What's that?" Susan asked.

"Dad must have sent us an e-mail. I have my computer set up to interrupt me if I get mail," Eric said. He pushed several buttons, and a message blinked onto the screen.

Susan, this is Dad. I have good news. Keep those grades up. I managed to get you on a special list of those eligible to enter a very upscale business school here on the East Coast when you graduate from high school. This is something I've been working on for several months. I hope you will be as excited as I am about it. When you get back to California, I'll call you with details. Love, Dad

Susan stared at the screen. Her shoulders slumped, and her forehead crinkled up.

"Um," Eric said. "How are you going to tell him about your mission to write books?"

"He won't understand," Susan said. "Maybe I could write in my free time and still go to the business school."

"You can't run away from your special mission. Besides, you know Dad. He believes in being focused on one thing. I don't think it would work," Eric said, looking at Susan.

"What can I do?" Susan said, brushing a tear from her cheek.

"Maybe we should talk to Dad more about our new ideas. Maybe he'll come to understand that God made us each different and that He has claims on our lives," Eric said. "Aunt Sally said that no one should force another person to do something, especially if God has told them not to."

"Do you think Dad would listen if I tried to explain that to him?" Susan asked.

"Of course. Here, let's send him a message right now," Eric said. "Just write a short letter, and I'll send it off."

Susan stared at the floor. *I don't know what to say,* she thought. *How can I tell Dad how much this whole experience means to me? I know it's the right thing. I just can't consider anything else. I wouldn't be happy. And what about obeying God and pleasing Him?*

"Go ahead. Just tell him how you feel," Eric urged.

Susan took a deep breath. "He'll think I'm too young to know my own mind," she objected. "Maybe that's true. Maybe I am too young."

"Age isn't the important thing. Lots of kids older than you don't know what they should be doing with their lives. Aunt Sally said that many people never figure it out. But you wanted to learn about God's plan for you, and you trusted Him to help you understand. He did, didn't He?"

"Yes," Susan said, sitting up straight. She looked at the screen for a moment and then she began to type.

Dear Dad,

Eric and I are learning a lot of new things. We want to talk with you about them. You know how happy Eric is since he has discovered his interest in photography. He might win a contest with his pictures at the Seven Seas Marine Institute.

Dad, I recently discovered something really great. God has given me a special ability to write. I love using words. I want to go to a college where I can learn to write. That's what I want to do when I grow up. Love, Susan

P.S. I've watched the sea creatures. Each one is different, and each has a special part to play in the reef system. And God created each one perfect for its part. I think He made people like that too.

Eric clicked the "Send" button, and the message disappeared. "He'll get it right away," Eric said. "Let's get back to the pictures. Don't worry—everything will be OK."

An hour later, just as a picture of three red Christmas worms popped onto the screen, a message interrupted them. "You have mail!" it said.

"That was quick," Eric said, clicking on the e-mail.

Hold everything, little lady. There will be no talk about you becoming a writer. I had this out with your mother years ago. She insisted on writing a book. I refused to help her print it, and I won't let you waste your life on writing either. Only someone who writes worthless novels makes any money. You need something solid that you can depend upon, so get that nonsense out of your head. There won't be one penny for your education unless you change your tune. We'll talk about the details of what I have planned for your schooling when you get home. Dad

Susan stared at the screen, and then she burst into tears. Eric patted her on the shoulder. He pushed the print button, and a copy of the e-mail popped out of the printer.

Eric picked up the printout of the e-mail, and Susan and he stared at the message again. "Imagine our mother being a writer," Susan said, a smile forming at the corners of her mouth. "I bet she was good."

Eric grabbed the book from the desk. He looked at the cover and then opened it. "This book was printed only two years ago," he said, looking at Susan. "Do you think this could be our mother's book? If Dad didn't want her to write, she might have used the pen name so he wouldn't find out."

"Eric, that's a wild idea," Susan said, reaching out and taking the book from him. She opened it and turned the pages. "There were four others with the name 'Judith Smith' on them. I found them hidden on the bottom shelf in Aunt Sally's office."

"What?" Eric shouted, staring at Susan and then at the book she held.

"They could all be Mother's," Susan said. Her eyes grew wide and her mouth flew open. "The note, Eric. I remember now. It was signed, 'Carol'!"

"I think we need to talk with Aunt Sally and Uncle Merle," Eric said, pulling Susan to her feet. "They'll know what to do."

Susan wiped her face and blew her nose. Then she and Eric stumbled down the stairs together. They found Uncle Merle in the kitchen, munching on a peanut-butter sandwich. "What's wrong?" he asked when he looked at them.

"We just got this e-mail from our father," Eric said, thrusting the paper into Uncle Merle's hands.

Uncle Merle read the message. "Sally, would you come into the kitchen for a moment please? I have something you need to take a look at."

When Aunt Sally entered the room, Uncle Merle handed her the paper. Aunt Sally read it and dropped onto a chair.

"I guess we're a little late," Uncle Merle said, looking at her.

"Eric thinks our mother wrote this book," Susan blurted, thrusting the book into Aunt Sally's hands and looking into her face. "Did she?"

"Yes, your mother wrote it," Aunt Sally said, running her hands over the cover. "There are four more in my bookcase at home."

"I love this book!" Susan said, taking the book back and holding it against her chest. "It makes me laugh and cry and want to go adventuring like the author . . . like my mother." Tears spilled down Susan's face. She couldn't stop them.

"Dad didn't want her to write them, did he?" Eric said. "That's why she used the pen name."

"Your father believed that writing is a waste of time. He forbade your mother to write, but she found small bits of time here and there. That's when she wrote those books. She begged me to help her, so we worked on the books together. Then I discovered that an author could get books published under a pen name. She was so happy when they were finally printed," Aunt Sally said, tears running down her cheeks. "I was so proud of her. She put a set of books aside for each of you."

"Oh," Susan said, sitting down beside Aunt Sally.

"She planned to talk with you about the books when you got a bit older. But, of course, she didn't get that opportunity."

Uncle Merle pulled Aunt Sally up into his arms. "That's done now," he said.

"Wow," Eric said, plopping onto the couch.

"This book is wonderful," Susan said. "Why should she have to hide a gift like that?"

"Perhaps she meant to keep peace in the family. But she just couldn't stop the words inside her from coming out," Aunt Sally said, turning toward the twins. "I wasn't trying to keep any of this from you. I'm sorry you had to find out this way."

"What will Susan do?" Eric asked. "She was born to write."

"I'm sure she was," Uncle Merle said. "We'll just have to talk with your father. We can explain what you have discovered and your view of God's leading. If he doesn't understand, then you'll have to make some tough decisions. But you have plenty of time. You must handle this carefully. Remember, while your father doesn't understand things the way you do, he is your father," he added.

"Sir," Eric said, standing up and squaring his shoulders. "I want to please my dad and show him respect, but I have to follow where God leads me. Susan will do the same thing. We need to pray about this. I feel sure God will help us."

Susan looked at Eric. She could see determination in his face. He looked so grown up. She dried her eyes. *I won't be discouraged*, she thought. *I know what God has shown me, and I know He'll have a solution.*

"I know it hurts," Aunt Sally said, "but give it some time. God has plans for your life. He will send the right help at the right time. We'll do everything we can to help."

"I think we should pray right now," Uncle Merle said. "Then it might be a good idea to spend some time diving."

Everyone knelt in a circle, holding hands. "Dear Father," Uncle Merle prayed, "it's so exciting to see the way You are opening Susan's understanding of her life mission. She knows that there will be difficulties, and she believes that You are ready to help her. Please help her father to consider her feelings and to support her as she chooses what she will do to serve You. And help Susan to trust You. Amen."

An hour later, they stood in the white sand looking out toward the reef. When they all had their BCDs on, they waded into the water. "Let's float out to the buoy that marks the reef," Uncle Merle said. "We can descend together as we always do."

"It feels good to be in the water," Susan said, just before she shoved her regulator into her mouth. Eric nodded his head yes and smiled.

Susan pumped air into her vest so she could float. She lay on her back and kicked. Thoughts of school and her future washed away on the small waves that passed beneath her.

"Add some more air to your vest, Susan," Uncle Merle said. "You're floating too low in the water."

Susan pushed a button and heard air enter her vest.

She continued to float, but in a few minutes, she felt herself settle deeper into the water. She pumped more air into her vest, but it didn't help.

"What's that weird sound?" Eric asked, moving up beside her.

"I don't know," Susan said, checking her gear.

"It sounds like you have a leak," Eric said. "Look at all the bubbles."

Susan spun around and noticed that bubbles were billowing out of her BCD. "You're right," she said calmly. "I do have a leak."

"Watch out!" Eric shouted. "If your vest bursts, you'll sink!"

"Hey, I've been through this before," Susan said. "Remember how my vest popped a leak when I was learning to SNUBA dive on Freedom Island? I thought I would drown—"

"But then I saved you," Eric said, grabbing at Susan.

"Don't worry, Eric," Susan said. "I'm OK; I still have plenty of air."

Eric signaled Aunt Sally and Uncle Merle, and Susan felt Uncle Merle grab the back of her vest and lift her up. Then Aunt Sally swam over and ran her fingers along the sides of Susan's vest. "You've got a leak right here," she said. "Every time you add air to your vest, it leaks out." Aunt Sally turned to Uncle Merle. "We need to head for shore," she said. "This leak could get worse very quickly."

When they climbed out of the water, Eric helped Susan remove her vest. "Boy, it's a good thing you sprang a leak so near to shore. Imagine what it would be like if—"

"Don't you love it, Sally, when equipment fails right near shore?" Uncle Merle interrupted, frowning at Eric.

"All we have to do is head for the dive shop. They'll be able to fix this up in no time."

"You two go ahead and dive," Aunt Sally said. "Susan and I will drive into town, get the vest repaired, and return with a big pizza."

"OK," Uncle Merle said. "Eric can concentrate on the sand flats right off shore—he hasn't taken many pictures there yet. We'll bask in the sun when we finish our dive."

"And we'll wait for that pizza!" Eric said.

"I love the way God is always looking after us when we dive," Aunt Sally said as she and Susan headed for town.

"It does feel good," Susan agreed. "I think He knew I would have been scared if my vest leaked while out in the middle of the sea. I'm determined to trust Him more and more," she said. "I'm getting plenty of practice."

Aunt Sally laughed. "It's the only way for a Christian to live. I'm so glad Jesus is such a trustworthy Friend. He knows how to take care of us even while we dive."

When they located the dive shop, Aunt Sally dried off the vest, and Susan carried it inside. "Hello," said a tall man who was wearing khaki shorts and a blue T-shirt. He fiddled with his bushy mustache and looked at the BCD in Susan's hand. "My name is Sammy," he said. "How may I help you today?"

"My vest has a leak," Susan said, holding up her BCD. "It shouldn't, because it's brand new. It burst right out in the ocean, sending a blast of bubbles everywhere."

"Wow! That must have scared you a bit. Look, you've got a tiny split in this seam," Sammy said. "Since it's a new vest, it should hold a repair without any problem. I don't have one like this in stock. You could go ahead and use it while you're here. Then, when you return home, you can return it for a brand-new one."

"That's what we'll do then. We have only a few days left to dive. Susan, I'll see to it that you get a new one when we get home," Aunt Sally said.

Susan and Aunt Sally headed for the pizza shop, leaving the vest at the store. When they returned, it hung on a hanger near the cash register. It looked like a bloated sea cucumber.

"It'll be ready for service tomorrow morning," Sammy said.

"Are you sure it won't split again?" Susan asked.

"I'm sure," he replied. Then he put pressure on the vest. Not a bit of air escaped.

"It's as good as new," Sammy said. He released the air from the vest. "If you wait till tomorrow, it'll be absolutely safe to use."

"Thank you," Aunt Sally said, taking the vest and heading for the car. Susan followed right behind her.

They parked the car, and Susan heard Eric shout, "They're here," as they headed down the small sand dune toward the beach. Aunt Sally spread a towel on the sand beneath a palm tree. "This pizza is still hot, Sally," Uncle Merle said, smiling. "You do work wonders."

"What about Susan's vest?" Eric asked, taking a bite of pizza.

"She'll be able to use it in the morning," Aunt Sally said.

That evening just before going to bed, Eric stopped at Susan's door. "I'm glad God showed you today that your vest needed repair," he said. "Tomorrow we're going to dive the wall."

The wall, Susan thought. *Not me. I'm not going out there. Sammy said my vest wouldn't burst, but what if it does?* Wild thoughts darted through her mind like the brittle stars that scampered away when she lifted rocks in the lagoon near the cottage. She stopped those thoughts in their tracks.

It's true that if my vest had burst while I hung off the wall eighty feet down, I might have been in deep trouble. Air would just have kept escaping until my tank emptied. I might have dropped down into the abyss. But it didn't burst there. God helped me when I needed it. I know I can trust Him. This is a good time to practice living what I choose to believe in my heart.

Susan got up. She grabbed her dive bag and looked at the gear list. She checked each piece of equipment as she added it to the bag. Then she placed her dive vest on top of the other gear. "I choose to go out to the wall. I choose not to be afraid," she said out loud. She hoped she would feel as brave in the morning as she did at that moment.

CHAPTER 9

DIVING THE WALL

The next morning, Susan and Eric plunked themselves into two chairs at the kitchen table, and Eric grabbed a cereal box. Uncle Merle stood in front of a window reading a sheet of paper. "What does it say, Merle?" Aunt Sally asked, sitting down beside Susan.

"This is definitely good news," Uncle Merle said, looking up. His face burst into a grin, and he looked straight at Eric.

"He won the contest!" Susan said, leaping to her feet. "I knew he would." She whirled around the kitchen, saying, "Eric won! Eric won!"

"Merle?" Aunt Sally said.

"Susan's right—he did win," Uncle Merle said, handing the paper to Aunt Sally.

Eric stared at Aunt Sally. She read, " 'Please have Eric contact me as soon as you return home. He will be honored at a special award ceremony a week from this Monday. I'll send more details later.' "

"Wow!" Eric said. "I didn't really think I could win."

"It seems that the committee chose you because of your photo skills and because of the unusual captions that

105

came with each picture," Aunt Sally said, looking up from the paper. "I guess that's why they call it a photo-journalism contest."

"The captions?" Eric said, frowning. "I—"

"This is wonderful, Eric!" Uncle Merle interrupted. "I'll let Mr. Wood know we will be returning in three days." He walked over to Eric and grasped his shoulder. "Well done," he said.

Susan smiled to herself. *I'm glad he won*, she thought.

"We'll enjoy looking at this every day," Aunt Sally said, placing the sheet of paper on the front of the refrigerator and slapping a small magnet against it.

"We certainly will," Uncle Merle said. He walked into the living room and looked out the window. "The sea is really calm today," he said. Everyone gathered around him. "It looks like a giant swimming pool. What do you say? Shall we go out to that wall?"

"Let's go!" they chorused.

An hour later, they stood, geared up, on the shore, looking out toward Babylon Reef. "I'm glad you never solved the boat problem, Aunt Sally," Eric said. "I've learned to love the time we spend swimming out to the dive sites."

"I like it, too," Susan said, "though sometimes I do wonder what might be swimming below me."

Aunt Sally and Uncle Merle laughed. "I can't believe we ever wondered if you would be able to take these long swims," Aunt Sally said.

"You already know the layout of the reef on the shallow side," Uncle Merle said. "The seaward side of the reef is a bit different." He opened his hand and spread out his fingers. "The shore side of the reef is like your wrist. Then it slopes at the palm of your hand to about fifty feet deep. At this point, the reef splits into fingers.

Between the fingers are deep trenches with sandy bottoms. We'll go over the reef and drop down into a trench, moving along toward the open sea. The whole reef system ends suddenly. At that point you can turn and look back at the reef wall."

Uncle Merle continued, "Stay with your dive partner. Aunt Sally will dive with Susan, and Eric, you will be with me. We'll go down the face of the wall no more than fifteen feet and stay no longer than fifteen minutes. Is all this clear?"

"Yes," Eric said, heading for the car. Susan followed.

"I can't wait to see what a wall looks like," Eric said, stowing his gear in the back of the station wagon.

"I hope it isn't dark or anything," Susan said. "But I have two lights with brand-new batteries just in case," she added. "Besides, they're a help even in the daytime. I can see the real colors of the sea creatures when I shine a light on them."

Susan couldn't believe her eyes when they arrived at the shore. The azure sea spread out before them like a giant, still tide pool.

The team swam on their backs to the first buoy. They stopped for a moment, but then Uncle Merle said, "We have to keep going until we reach that buoy farther out."

Susan started kicking her fins again. She didn't hurry. *Diving isn't about hurrying*, she reminded herself. *It's about lingering and snooping around.*

When they reached the second buoy, they descended to the sunlit reef and turned toward the open sea. They passed over the garden of corals where a school of yellowtail snappers swirled around and a shy queen angelfish peeked at them from behind a sea fan. Soon they reached the beginning of a trench. Uncle Merle dropped down slowly, and Susan, Eric, and Aunt Sally followed. They sank down between ragged, gray walls that squeezed closer together near the top, almost shutting out the light above them. When the trench narrowed, they swam along single file. Susan glanced at her depth gauge as she neared the sandy bottom. It said sixty-five feet.

Suddenly, her arm began to burn as if she had bumped a hot stove. "Ouch!" she yelled through her regulator. *Something with stinging nematocyst cells got me*, she thought. She turned her arm so she could see. It looked red and swollen. She remembered not to rub the area because that would only push the cells into her flesh. Aunt Sally stopped and looked at her. "Are you OK?" she asked, using the dive sign.

"I'm OK," Susan signaled, making a circle with her thumb and first finger. Soon the sting began to ease a bit. She looked up. Strands of whiplike creatures hung out over the trench. *One of those guys got me*, she thought, moving along more carefully to avoid several others that stuck out from the coral wall.

Aunt Sally and Susan continued through the trench. When Uncle Merle reached the end of the trench and swam into the open water, he turned and motioned for the others to join him. Eric swam out and looked back at them. Susan saw his face light up like a lighthouse lamp. He flashed her a smile and waved for her to hurry up. She kicked her fins, burst out of the trench, and hung suspended over nothing.

She whirled around and looked at the reef. It ended suddenly in a great wall that plunged down into darkness. Susan gasped, and her stomach knotted up. She looked up through sixty-five feet of water. It brightened as it went up, but she couldn't see the surface. She looked down. The water grew darker and darker, deepening quickly into total blackness.

Aunt Sally swam up beside her. She pulled out her dive slate and wrote, "There's almost six thousand feet of water below you." Susan grabbed Aunt Sally. *I'm going to sink away into the abyss,* she thought, and a chill ran up and down her spine. But she didn't sink, and she could see that Aunt Sally wore a smile. *She isn't afraid,* Susan thought.

They hung in the water, staring at the giant wall formation. *I feel like a star shining in the night sky*, she thought. *I'm hanging here, weightless and silent—a tiny speck.*

Susan looked at Aunt Sally, and she smiled back. Susan saw trickles of water seep into Aunt Sally's mask. Soon an inch of water sloshed in the bottom of it, just below her eyes. Susan pointed to her mask. Aunt Sally shrugged. She held her right hand against her mask and pressed. Then she blew air out her nose into the mask. The water disappeared. *It's a good thing we learned to clear our mask deep in the sea. Every time Aunt Sally smiles, water trickles into the sides of her mask,* she thought.

Susan gave Aunt Sally the OK signal and they moved, with Uncle Merle and Eric, closer to the wall. Susan watched Eric dart this way and that, clicking his camera. *He's the one in a hurry this time,* she thought. *He's trying to get as many pictures as he can in a short time.*

She began to explore. She spotted a cluster of giant tube sponges jutting out into the sea, their hungry mouths sipping up particles of animal and plant plankton that passed by. She swam over and looked into the opening in a pink vase sponge that clutched a rock nearby. Two hairy brittle stars clung to the inside walls. She clicked on her dive light and pointed it into the sponge's opening. A red light glowed through the sponge—she could see the outline of the brittle star clearly. Eric moved over and snapped some pictures.

Susan let herself sink a few feet down the wall. A deep-water sea fan had glued itself to an old coral head and had grown to be larger than Susan. It hung off the side of the wall, waving back and forth in the gentle current. *It looks like a lacy skeleton spread out against the dark water,* she thought, letting herself sink down. She had descended only a little when Aunt Sally nudged her, signaling her to go up.

When she ascended a few feet, she found herself staring at a boulder brain coral. Her eyes focused on two purple, top-shaped creatures sticking out of it. They looked like miniature feather dusters. When she drew near, the creatures spiraled around and around, disappearing into tiny holes almost before she could blink her eyes. Aunt Sally reached for her dive slate. "Christmas tree worms," she wrote on it.

After a few moments, the worms popped out of their holes. Susan waved her hands over them, and they dropped out of sight in a flash. Susan laughed, and she looked at Aunt Sally. Her eyes laughed, but she kept her face still. *She's trying not to laugh and get water in her mask again,* Susan thought.

They spotted a cleaning station manned by two banded coral shrimp dressed in red-and-white-striped suits. The shrimp pranced on tiny white claws over a great barracuda that was wearing black stripes on its gray sides that signaled its readiness to be cleaned. The shrimp waved long antennae about as they snipped tiny parasites from the barracuda. When they passed a small crevice, a green moray eel poked its head out. *It looks like an old man with his mouth agape who has lost his dentures,* Susan thought.

Way too soon, Aunt Sally motioned for Susan to follow her. They moved to the top of the reef and turned and peered over the edge at Eric and Uncle Merle. For some reason, Susan felt safer with the reef beneath her, yet she longed to go down the wall and explore it more.

Suddenly, a big sea turtle zoomed up from the abyss, heading straight for Eric and Uncle Merle, who still hung in front of the wall. Eric managed to point his camera at the turtle and snap a picture. The turtle saw the light flash, took one look at Eric and then turned away and headed for the reef top, where Susan and Aunt Sally lay.

Susan smiled. *I'm going to see a turtle up close,* she thought.

The turtle didn't see her. It just kept coming, and then it was in her face. She could see the folds of white, smooth skin that encircled its neck, the large black spots on its front flippers, and its sharp, hooked beak. She almost fell over backwards to keep the turtle from smashing into her. Finally, the turtle saw her. It made a U-turn and sped away. Eric trailed after it, but he didn't go far. Susan saw him hurry back to the sunny reef. She didn't blame him. *There is just too much dark, deep water out there with no bottom in sight,* she thought.

They lingered on the reef for twenty minutes more. Susan looked into crevices and dozens of tiny holes. Each held a treasure that made her smile. She took a deep breath and moved backwards when a trumpetfish darted out from the branches of a gorgonian where it had been standing on its head, hiding from predators.

The reef is wonderful, Susan thought, looking around at the spectacle before her. *God's family is just like this reef. Every person has a special role and is unique and different. And I'm part of this family, now.* Susan sighed. How could she ever explain to her father what she had seen in the world beneath the sea and how much it meant to her? How could she tell him how visiting the reef, especially the wall, had changed her? She lay still, trying to memorize each color and shape.

Eventually, Aunt Sally motioned for her to follow again. They headed across the corals and followed the gentle slope up to the shallow side of the reef. It gradually thinned out into scattered coral formations and then into a sandy field that ended at the shore.

"I have to go back soon," Susan said as she struggled out of the water.

"Me too," Eric said.

Aunt Sally and Uncle Merle laughed. "I think we started something," Uncle Merle said.

"Yes, we did," Aunt Sally agreed. "I understand. My thoughts are never far from the reef—even when I'm sitting in a dry room miles from the sea."

"What makes it all so magical?" Susan asked when they had gathered around the kitchen table that evening. She felt sure she would never be the same again—never be completely happy on dry land.

"Perhaps it's an almost unspoiled world that pulsates with life," Uncle Merle said, grabbing a sandwich from the plate in the center of the table.

Aunt Sally said, "All kinds of creatures swirl all around me out there. It's so exciting. But that isn't what draws me back again and again. I go back because I always feel close to my Creator when I'm down there gazing at the reef."

Everyone agreed. They sat quietly for several minutes, lost in the memory of the reef.

"Every creature knows what its role in the reef is," Eric said suddenly. "You would never see a sponge uproot itself and march over to a cleaning station so it could become a cleaner."

Susan laughed at the picture in her mind of a clumsy sponge, with no pinchers, stumbling around a cleaner station. Then, suddenly, she looked sad. "But people do that," she said, sniffling. "They become things they don't want to become and do things they aren't suited for."

"Or other people push them into situations like that," Eric said, looking at Susan.

"Why do they do it?" Susan sobbed. "Why?"

Aunt Sally moved next to Susan. "They just don't understand God and how He is leading in another person's life," she said, smoothing Susan's hair back from her face.

"I believe that threatening or forcing someone to live a life he or she isn't meant to live is a crime," Uncle Merle said. "It shows lack of respect for that person, a lack of valuing what God has made that person to be. It's a thoughtless rebellion against the Creator's desires and plans. I've seen too many people hurt by that." While he spoke, he was looking at Aunt Sally.

The twins stared at Uncle Merle. He usually stayed calm even when everyone else became upset, but right then his face looked like a storm cloud. "They could understand if they wanted to," he added, his face bunched up into a frown. "The Bible teaches us the truth about this."

"I'm glad we're beginning to understand," Susan said, wiping her eyes. "We have to be patient with those who don't, I guess," she said, sighing, "But we have to follow the truth in spite of what they say or do."

"That isn't easy," Eric said.

"Well, it wouldn't be easy to go against what you know to be right either," Susan said. "How could a sponge clean parasites off a fish?"

"I guess that wouldn't work," Eric admitted.

"We're all being gloomy-heads about this," Aunt Sally said, her face brightening. "We need to remember who is in charge here. Our God knows how to help us through difficult situations. We don't have to be afraid."

"Of course, you're right," Uncle Merle said. "You knobby-heads don't have a thing to worry about. You've put God in charge of your lives."

A smile erased Eric's frown, and Susan laughed. She liked the name Uncle Merle had called them. She realized that he really cared about their happiness. Right at that moment she determined to keep walking along the path God was mapping out for her. *When I don't get it or have times of confusion, I'll just wait for God to show me more,* she said to herself.

"Isaiah said something about this to God," Uncle Merle said. " 'You are the one we trust to bring about justice; above all else we want your name to be honored' " (Isaiah 26:8).

"Wow," Eric said. "That's what I want to say."

"The fourth verse in that chapter says, 'So always trust in the LORD because he is forever our mighty rock,' " Aunt Sally added.

Eric reached out and picked up a Bible that sat nearby. He leafed through it until he found the book of Isaiah. He turned the pages slowly, scanning the words.

"Look at this," he said. " 'This wonderful knowledge comes from the LORD All-Powerful, who has such great wisdom.' That's verse twenty-nine in chapter twenty-eight."

Susan moved over to Eric's side. She stared at the page as Eric turned it. "Stop," she said. "Look at verses eighteen and nineteen in the thirtieth chapter."

"Read it, Susan," Uncle Merle suggested.

" 'The LORD God is waiting to show how kind he is and to have pity on you. The LORD always does right; He blesses those who trust him. People of Jerusalem, you don't need to cry anymore. The Lord is kind, and as soon as he hears your cries for help, he will come.' "

Susan looked up and brushed a tear off her cheek.

"I'm glad I chose Him to be my Savior," Eric said, closing the Bible and standing up. "Anyone who can make a reef like I saw today and keep it all working can certainly take care of me and show me how I fit into His plan." He tucked the Bible under his arm and headed up the stairs to his room. Susan smiled at Aunt Sally and Uncle Merle and followed Eric.

"Why are you leaving in such a hurry?" she asked, coming up behind him.

"I want to see what else this Isaiah guy has to say. He seems really smart to me," Eric said, disappearing into his room.

"Please tell me tomorrow what you discover," Susan called after him. She felt relieved that Eric hadn't asked her to work on pictures. *I have a lot to think over,* she thought. *I might have to face some stormy seas ahead. Good thing God is like a good BCD.*

When Susan showered, she washed the salt away but not the memory of the reef. When she climbed into bed, she could see Eric's light shining out through the crack under his door. She sighed and thought, *He's still reading.* Then she fell asleep, dreaming of signing her name to her first book—though she had to admit to herself that she didn't know how it would ever happen. *God knows,* she thought, and she fell asleep.

CHAPTER 10

SUSAN'S TRIUMPH

For the next two days, they dived the wall. The mystery and beauty of it wrapped itself around their hearts. They watched spotted eagle rays soar, shrimp dance, and sea stars creep.

"We may have to go home tomorrow, but I'm coming back soon," Eric said, looking at Susan as they climbed out of the water and headed for the car after their last day of diving.

"Not without me," she said.

As they drove away, images of fantastic creatures that paraded through the reef remained in their minds. "I'm glad we have pictures. I'm going to look at them a lot when we get home," Susan said.

The next morning, Eric said, "We can't SCUBA dive today. We have to breathe out all the nitrogen stored in our bodies. Uncle Merle said it's a safety rule. No diving for twenty-four hours before flying." So, they helped Aunt Sally and Uncle Merle collect and pack the things they'd need to bring back home with them.

After lunch, Susan found Eric in his room, stuffing clothes into a suitcase. He picked up a stack of books and started to put them in his suitcase too. Then Susan spotted the picture of a sea creature on the front of one of the books. She grabbed the book and cried, "It's him!"

"Who?" Eric said, staring at Susan.

"I saw this creature," Susan said, pointing to the book cover.

"When did you see a manta ray?" Eric said. "We didn't see one when we were diving. We saw southern stingrays. They're a whole lot smaller than this giant."

Susan opened the book and flipped several pages. A flat, black creature with large wings and two small arms on each side of its huge, open mouth stared at her. "Manta Ray," the caption read. Susan's eyes opened wide. "It eats plankton," she said. "It never eats big creatures. Never! I thought it was going to eat me," she said, looking up at Eric. "I thought—"

"You really mean it? You saw that creature?" he said.

"I went for a walk our first morning here," Susan explained. "I put on my mask and waded into the shallow water to look around."

"You got into the water alone?" Eric said, staring at her. "You know the rule—"

"I know," Susan interrupted. "I only meant to lie there for a minute. Then the sky went black, the water got dark, and this huge creature just cruised up to me. It started scooping water into its mouth. I thought it was going to scoop me in too. I was terrified."

"Wow!" Eric said.

"But it says here that although manta rays are powerful giants, they are gentle and won't hurt a diver," Susan said, looking down at the page. "And all this time I was scared of meeting up with another one out there somewhere."

Eric stared out the window and shook his head. "You never said anything about it," he said.

"I wanted to forget," Susan admitted. "I knew if I didn't, I'd never go into the water again. I meant to search our books for its picture, but I never found the time. I sure wish I knew then what I know now."

"Wow," Eric said again. "I used to think of God like you thought about the manta ray. I knew He was powerful. What I didn't know was that He loved me and meant to help me, not to hurt me."

Then Eric grabbed Susan by the hand and picked up his camera. "Show me where you saw the ray," he said. "Maybe we could see it again."

"There isn't much chance of that, but it can't hurt to try," she said, setting the book down.

They collected their snorkel gear and headed for the spot where the manta ray had scared Susan weeks earlier. When they had their gear on and were in the water, Susan said, "Just lie still. Maybe it returns here to feed every day."

Long minutes passed, and the afternoon sun sank toward the horizon. Suddenly, the water darkened. Susan looked up. A black creature soared toward them, staring at them. Eric snapped a picture and then they moved as close as they dared to the giant. Susan didn't feel afraid. She looked at Eric. His eyes shone with excitement.

The manta ray swam in front of them and then turned and cruised past again. It scooped water into its huge, open mouth. Eric tugged at Susan, and they moved closer. All at once, the great creature turned and swept out toward the distant reef, its long dagger tail trailing behind.

"Wow!" Eric said, standing up.

"It was so different," Susan said, popping up beside him. "This time I wasn't afraid because I know the truth about manta rays. Instead of thrashing around and trying to escape, I just stayed still and looked closer. Maybe facing trouble is like that. When it moves in and blacks out our joy like the manta ray blocked the sun, we panic."

"Did you panic the day you saw it?" Eric asked.

Susan ignored his question. "When we understand the truth—that God is right there to help us—we can stay calm and look for a solution," she said.

"If you had asked me, I could have told you the truth about the harmless manta ray and saved you a lot of trouble," Eric said.

Susan laughed. "Let's go," she said. The twins waded out of the water and headed for the cottage. "I guess we better finish packing," Eric said, but Susan knew he'd spend some time downloading the pictures first.

The next morning, they boarded the airplane for home. From the airplane window, Grand Cayman island looked like a green gem ringed with white and surrounded by endless blue. Susan waved goodbye, promising herself that she would return. She would look for the manta ray, the turtles, and even the scary eels.

When they reached Laguna Beach after two long days of travel, they cleaned and stowed their gear. Susan smiled every time she remembered the creatures she had met in the reef.

The next day, Aunt Sally called up the stairs, "Eric, you have a telegram."

Susan followed Eric down the stairs. "It's from Mr. Wood," he said. He opened the envelope, and everyone stared at Eric, waiting.

"I have to be at the Seven Seas Marine Institute tomorrow evening at six to receive the award," Eric said, handing the telegram back to Aunt Sally.

"This is so exciting," Susan said, jumping around.

Then the phone rang. Uncle Merle answered it. "Yes, Frank. The kids are here," Susan heard him say. Eric grabbed an extension, and Uncle Merle handed his phone to Susan.

"I'm glad you're home safe," the familiar voice of their father said. "Now, Susan, I hope you've thought over my e-mail. I haven't changed my mind. I've set aside money so you can go to college. I have no intention of allowing you to . . ."

Susan listened to her father's words. She tried to hold on to her joy, but his words covered her like a black cloud. She felt as though she were suddenly facing something terrible that could hurt her. She started to panic, but then she remembered the manta ray and her decision.

"Dad, I'm glad you called," she said. "I haven't changed my mind. I'm going to get a degree in creative writing. I've learned a lot from the sea creatures, and I want to use what I've learned to help people know God better. I'll need your help."

Susan heard Eric suck in his breath. She smiled over at him and gave him the dive sign for OK. There was a long silence on the phone.

"Susan. If you decide to do that, I won't give you a penny. That's final. Not one cent. You have three years to get this nonsense out of your head. Do you hear me?" her father said.

"I hear you, Dad," Susan said. But she didn't hear any more words. *I know God loves me and will help me find a solution,* she thought. *I'm not going to be afraid.*

"You were brave," Eric said when they hung up. "Dad isn't going to change his mind, ever."

"I know," Susan said, turning and heading for her room.

The next day overflowed with activity. They finished unpacking, shopped for groceries, and picked up school supplies.

That evening, Susan found herself seated with Uncle Merle, Aunt Sally, and Eric in a row of chairs at the Seven Seas Marine Institute. Her thoughts turned to the problem of school. *How will I ever earn enough money to go to college?* she wondered.

Then the overhead lights blinked off, and Mr. Wood and six other adults walked onto the lighted stage. Susan pulled her thoughts together and focused on what a man behind the podium was saying. "We've gathered here tonight to review the good work of the institute for the previous year and to unveil our plans for the future." The man smoothed his beard with one hand and then shuffled some papers. "We will also announce the winner of our annual photo journalism contest."

Susan looked over at Eric and smiled. He stared at the stage, and beads of sweat formed on his forehead. He wiped them off and looked down at his feet.

Susan listened to the speeches and joined others when they clapped. Time dragged by. Then Mr. Wood stood up. Susan stared. He looked different in his suit and black dress shoes.

"I now have the pleasure of announcing the winner of the Seven Seas Marine Photo Journalism Contest," Mr. Wood said, and a big smile lighted up his tanned face. "Eric, will you please come forward."

The crowd burst into applause. Aunt Sally nudged Eric from his seat and walked with him down the aisle and onto the stage. Susan smiled when Eric smoothed a shock of blond hair with his hand. He fidgeted and stared at his feet.

"Eric," Mr. Wood said, "the Seven Seas Marine Institute wishes to recognize and encourage young talent in photo journalism. Your work in underwater photography has been recognized as superior in composition, clarity, and interest. Each picture you submitted told a story—especially the one of your sister, Susan, leaping out of the sea with a red octopus on her mask." The picture popped onto the screen behind the stage. Susan gasped, and everyone else burst into laughter.

Each picture that Eric had submitted appeared on screen, along with the captions. Susan noticed that Eric stared at the screen and jammed his hands deep into his pockets.

When the people quieted, Mr. Wood continued. "In part, you have been selected as our winner because of the fine, vibrant descriptions that you included with each picture. Because you show great enthusiasm and desire to continue to develop these fine skills, we congratulate you as the winner of the Seven Seas Marine Photo Journalism Award," he said, reaching out his hand to Eric. "This prize includes an award of twenty thousand dollars for four years of education at a college of your choice."

Susan sucked in her breath, and the crowd erupted in clapping. But Eric stood silent. He didn't hold out his hand.

"Eric?" Mr. Wood said when everyone settled down.

"I didn't write the captions—she did," Eric blurted, pointing to Susan.

Silence filled the room. Everyone turned to stare at Susan.

"Eric, are you saying that you had help with the journalism portion of the contest?" Mr. Wood said.

"No, sir," Eric said. "My captions were terrible. I knew they were. But no one helped me improve them. My sister changed them all. I didn't realize it until I saw them on the screen just now. They aren't mine. Not one of them." He turned to walk off the stage.

"Just a minute, son," Mr. Wood said. He turned to the others on the stage, and they huddled together and talked. Susan slunk down in her chair.

In a few moments, Mr. Wood returned to the microphone. "Well," he said, clearing his throat, "we've had quite a surprise here tonight. Our committee has agreed that a mistake has been made."

Susan groaned. She looked at Eric. His face went beet red. He wiped his face with his hand and looked at the floor.

Susan wanted to do something, but she couldn't think of anything. Suddenly, she stood up. "It's my fault," she blurted. "I changed all the captions because they were boring. Eric didn't ask me to. He just asked me to look at the pictures. I didn't tell him I changed all the words."

The people sat in silence for a long moment. "Young lady, please come up here," Mr. Wood said, motioning to Susan. Hundreds of eyes turned to stare at her. Uncle Merle stood up and walked with her to the platform.

"As I said," Mr. Wood continued, "our committee has agreed that we made a mistake. Instead of one talented young person, we admit that we have discovered two of them. They acted as a team. Our mistake seems to be that we thought the two skills would naturally appear in one person. However, Susan and Eric have shown us that these two skills, writing and photography, are often found in separate people. And when these two skills are put together, the result is wonderful."

He understands, Susan thought. She smiled at Eric, who looked as relieved as when the sleeping shark they had spotted in the cave on the reef didn't wake up. He gave Susan a weak smile.

"Therefore, we have decided," Mr. Wood continued,

"to give both Susan and Eric a first-place award of twenty thousand dollars each for their future education."

The audience stood to their feet and applauded. Uncle Merle hugged Susan, and Aunt Sally grabbed Eric's hand. A man who was sitting on the platform scribbled something on a small slip of paper and handed it to Mr. Wood. He tucked it into the envelope that he held and handed it to Susan.

"Thank you," the twins chorused and then they returned to their seats.

Susan sat down and opened the envelope. When she saw two checks for twenty thousand dollars in it, she sighed. *It won't pay for my education, but it's a start. God is already working in my behalf,* she thought, and she felt peace sweep over her. Then she held up Eric's check and smiled at him.

They enjoyed the refreshments that followed and meeting many people who wished them well in their future projects. But Susan kept thinking of the way God had started to open doors for her. She felt excited.

As they climbed into the car to go home, Aunt Sally said, "Eric, I'm proud of what you did tonight," and she wiped her eyes.

"Thank you, Eric," Susan said.

"Son," Uncle Merle said, "you did the right thing. But you sure had me scared for a moment there." Everyone laughed. "I think you've begun to see how God works to help those who turn to Him and who choose to do right."

When they entered the house, Aunt Sally picked up a stack of mail, and Susan and Eric started up the stairs to their rooms.

Aunt Sally sat down and tore open an envelope. "Hold it," she said, looking up from a letter she held in her hands. She continued to read for a moment and then stood up, tears streaming from her eyes.

"What's wrong now?" Uncle Merle asked, moving to her side and handing her a handkerchief. "Is it bad news?"

"No, no," Aunt Sally sobbed. "It isn't bad news."

Uncle Merle took the letter and read it silently. Susan and Eric stared at Aunt Sally and then at Uncle Merle. He looked up at the twins and smiled. "Come, sit down," he said, ushering them into the living room. "Our God has been at work again."

"What do you mean?" Susan and Eric chorused.

"Susan," Aunt Sally said, sniffling, "Do you remember giving me the note that fell from your mother's book?"

"Yes," Susan said.

"You didn't read the whole note," Aunt Sally said, wiping her eyes.

"I didn't. Honestly, I didn't," Susan blurted, jumping up and joining Aunt Sally on the couch.

"That's why you don't know what a wonderful thing has just happened," Aunt Sally said, laughing.

"What happened?" Eric asked, looking from Susan to Aunt Sally. "What does that letter have to do with a note that everyone is so excited about?"

"This is a letter from Mr. Store. He's a lawyer. Your mother hired him to set up a trust for you both. She set aside the income from her books—the royalties—for your education."

Susan stared at Eric.

"Wow!" Eric said.

"But what school do we have to go to?" Susan asked. *Even if I can't accept Mother's help and it hurts a lot,* she thought, *I choose to do what God is leading me to do.* Then

Susan realized that her heart was set. She felt a sense of triumph. She had won. No matter what or who pressured her, no matter how much good or harm they meant to do, she would listen to God and obey Him. She pressed her lips together.

"Susan, you don't understand. You can choose any school you want. The money has already collected interest and will continue to do so. By the time you need it, there will be plenty of money to cover your education," Aunt Sally said, bursting into tears again.

"You mean I can become a writer?" Susan asked, tears spilling over her cheeks.

"Our mother understood, didn't she," Eric said.

"Yes," Aunt Sally said. "She understood, and she found a way to help you."

"God understands too," Eric said. "He sent help even before we needed it. We trusted Him, and we made the right choice."

"This is the way God chose to help us, Eric," Susan said. "I believe He will find a way to help other young people who turn to Him and trust Him. We can use our gifts to help them learn about what God is really like so they will see that He is Someone they can trust."

"I think you both have work to do over the next three years," Uncle Merle said, his face breaking into one of his famous grins.

"We'll study hard," Eric said.

"We will—except when we're diving into the great, blue sea," Susan said.

IF YOU ENJOYED THIS BOOK, YOU'LL ENJOY THESE ALSO.

Summer of the Sharks
Sally Streib

Spend the summer with twins Susan and Eric and their friend, Kevin, swimming, snorkeling, and SNUBA diving in a dazzling undersea world of wonder and beauty. But it is a world of danger as well. Sharks lurk in the water, accidents can happen, and someone will need rescuing. Will Eric trust God to help him overcome his fears and keep him from harm? (Ages 10–14) Paperback, 128 pages. 0-8163-2126-4 US$7.99

Shepherd Warrior
Bradley Booth

What is it like to go and fight? David wondered as he watched his older brothers leave to war against the Philistines. He would stay behind and tend to the needs of his father's sheep. But God had many plans for this young man. (Ages 10–14) Paperback, 128 pages. 0-8163-2161-2 US$10.99

Escape!
Sandy Zaugg

"Get out of Haynau today!" shouted a German soldier. "The Russian army is on its way!" This is the true story of Dieter, a thirteen-year-old German boy, and his mother who fled their home near the end of World War II with only what they could carry on their bicycles. (Ages 9–13) Paperback, 96 pages. 0-8163-2140-X US$9.99